SIDO KANHU

'It is now becoming increasingly obvious that, unfortunately, India's established historians post Independence were heavily influenced by British colonial biases. Their historiography was guided more by the perspective of the invaders and less by us native Indians. Therefore, it is no surprise that many important parts of Indian history were ignored. A very significant one is the inspiring rebellion of the brave Sido Murmu and Kanhu Murmu against British colonial oppression. I'm almost certain that this is one of the most inspiring stories that you have never been told about. The Santhal War of 1855 is a story that had to be told, and I'm glad it's being told with such stark vividness and raw emotion. Read it, and honour those who fought on the side of India against foreign oppression.'

—**Amish**
Author and Director, Nehru Centre, London

SIDO KANHU

The *Santhal Hul*, Bharat's First War of Independence

TUHIN A. SINHA
CLARK PRASAD

Published by
Rupa Publications India Pvt. Ltd 2023
7/16, Ansari Road, Daryaganj
New Delhi 110002

Sales Centres:
Prayagraj Bengaluru Chennai
Hyderabad Jaipur Kathmandu
Kolkata Mumbai

Copyright © Tuhin A. Sinha and Suraj Prasad

The views and opinions expressed in this book are the authors' own and the facts are as reported by them which have been verified to the extent possible, and the publishers are not in any way liable for the same.

All rights reserved.

No part of this publication may be reproduced, transmitted, or stored in a retrieval system, in any form or by any means, electronic, mechanical, photocopying, recording or otherwise, without the prior permission of the publisher.

P-ISBN: 978-93-5702-286-6
E-ISBN: 978-93-5702-277-4

First impression 2023

10 9 8 7 6 5 4 3 2 1

Printed in India

This book is sold subject to the condition that it shall not, by way of trade or otherwise, be lent, resold, hired out, or otherwise circulated, without the publisher's prior consent, in any form of binding or cover other than that in which it is published

*To the seventy lakh Santhals of Bharat, whose forefathers
led an epic revolution for independence, of which
the present generation knows very little*

Charles Dickens
Courtesy: Wikimedia Commons

'There seems also to be a sentiment of honour among them; for it is said that they use poisoned arrows in hunting, but never against their foes. If this be the case—and we hear nothing of poisoned arrows in the recent conflicts—they are infinitely more respectable than our civilised enemy.'

Charles Dickens, in an entry on the Santhals in his weekly magazine *Household Words* (Volume XII, p. 349)

INTRODUCTION

While the Revolt of 1857 is known to every Indian school-going child and is invariably referred to as our first war of independence, the Indian freedom movement really has more facets to it than has been covered in detail till date. Subaltern uprisings against the British predate the mainstream freedom movement that has been covered and of which we usually talk. Post Independence, the colonial hangover of our historians continued for several decades, making any consequential course correction difficult. However, as India is evolving as a nation, it is important to dig deeper into the world of those whose contributions to the nation's journey has hitherto been overlooked.

When author Tuhin A. Sinha first started working on the story of Birsa Munda a few years ago, in no time, he was drawn into the complex world of our tribal heroes. The novel was followed by a collection of essays on 17 of our greatest tribal warriors across the country. This book, *Sido Kanhu*, co-authored with Clark Prasad (Suraj Prasad), is based on the Santhal Insurrection of 1855.

Before delving further, it is important to learn about the land of the Santhals, a proud ethnic group spread between the present-day areas of Bhagalpur and Purnea in Bihar, the northern parts of Jharkhand and the fields of adjoining West Bengal. Of course, this entire land came under the erstwhile Bengal province in the nineteenth century.

To truly appreciate the Santhals' story, it is imperative to understand the history of the region. After the Battle of Plassey in 1757, the East India Company emerged victorious over the Nawab of Bengal, Siraj ud-Daulah, paving the way for it to take control of erstwhile Bengal. In 1793, the introduction of the Permanent Settlement Act fixed the land revenue payable by zamindars. In effect, it meant increasing farm productivity, which resulted in the oppression of the peasants across Bengal at the hands of the zamindars.

But the Santhals, a people with a rich history and culture, refused to let themselves be crushed under the weight of colonial rule. While poverty had reduced them to being a migrant population within the region, they longed for a semblance of permanence in their lives. Fast-forward to the year 1832—we reach the time when the British carved out a land known as Damin-i-koh in the Rajmahal Hills of Jharkhand. Apart from a small number of Pahariyas—the original inhabitants—they started settling the Santhals there in large numbers. The Santhals felt at home in the dense forests and naturally fell in love with the land. They saw Damin-i-koh as their promised land, where they could thrive and maintain their way of life. But the British and the zamindars merely saw them as tools to increase their wealth, exploiting their skills in forest clearing and cultivation and subsequently imposing costs that the Santhals were not willing to pay. The basic conflict of *jal, jungle and zameen* (water, forests and land) only aggravated over the years when cleared forests were given to non-local zamindars for cultivation. The Santhals would always end up feeling cheated and used. Over the years, it led to retaliation and revolt.

Unlike the well-documented mainstream freedom movement, the tribal revolts were far more layered. The British would invariably outsource their control in subaltern parts to the landlords or zamindars. The stiff revenue targets handed over to zamindars had them unleash atrocities upon the peasants. Post 1850, Christian missionaries were gradually introduced in many of these areas to proselytize the poor tribals. With the zamindars as their primary interface, the tribals seldom had a direct engagement with the British.

An interesting part of the 1855 Santhal Insurrection is that while nearly 50,000 Santhals are said to have participated in it and 10,000 died over a period of almost eight to nine months, it was primarily aimed against the wily pro-British zamindars when it started. The Santhals had no idea about the resources of the British—they lived in a closed world of their own. At the same time, the British were equally taken aback by the magnitude of the revolt as very few of their officers knew the region or the people well.

The Santhal Hul was eastern India's biggest uprising against the British. The simultaneous playout of the 1857 revolt across the country caught the attention of the world. Had it not been for this uprising, the Santhal Hul would have been regarded as India's first war of independence. Also, it is believed that many of the sepoys involved in crushing the revolution died in the 1857 revolt—one of the reasons why the facts involving the Santhal Hul did not get documented for a long time.

The Santhal Hul left its impact on the years to come. Quoting from Tuhin A. Sinha's book *The Great Tribal Warriors of Bharat*, co-authored with Ambalika,

> As the Hul ended, Ashley Eden, who later went on to become the lieutenant governor of Bengal, launched an enquiry to understand why this uprising had come as a surprise. Much to the astonishment of the government, its officers realized that the Santhals were right—there was no effective means of dispensing justice and the economy did consist of administering taxes without offering anything substantial in return. Based on these findings, the Sonthal Parganas Act (Act XXXVII) of 1855 was introduced. The Act consolidated the Santhal areas into a separate non regulation district—the Santhal Parganas. This area was separated from the districts of Bhagalpur and Birbhum and divided into four sub districts—Dumka, Deodhar, Godda and Rajmahal (including Pakur). Eden went on to become the first deputy commissioner of Santhal Parganas, after which he introduced the Police Rules of 1856, which invested the majhis of the Santhal villages with police powers that they could exercise in their villages, assisted by the village chowkidar.*

---

*Sinha, Tuhin A. and Ambalika, *The Great Tribal Warriors of Bharat*, Rupa Publications, 2022.

Sido Kanhu is a celebration of the bravery of a Santhal Murmu family—the four brothers, Sido, Kanhu, Chand and Bhairab, and their two sisters, Phulo and Jano—the architects of what will remain one of Bharat's biggest subaltern uprising against the British, both in terms of its geography and impact. This book is a testament to the complexities and nuances of India's struggle for independence, and a beacon of hope for all those who seek to break free from oppression and reclaim their liberty. The Santhals' story is a reminder that even the smallest group of people can stand up to the mightiest of empires.

The book is a dramatized recreation based on historical facts.

In the process of writing the book, the authors have referred to various credible sources to authenticate that period in history.

PROLOGUE

December 1852
Kalikata, Capital of East India Company
British India

As the first rays of the sun crept over the horizon, the silence of Kalighat was pierced by the shuffling of feet. The pilgrims had arrived at the towering temple of Kali, their voices hushed in reverence as they gazed upon the ancient red-stoned walls. From all corners of the city, countryside and beyond, they had journeyed to this holy ground to pay homage to the goddess of death, time and doomsday.

The entrance to the temple was guarded by a high wall, its surface adorned with fragrant garlands of marigold and jasmine. A sweet scent filled the air, a symbol of the sacredness of the space that lay beyond. Within the temple, devotees made offerings and lit incense sticks. The smoke from the burning incense rose in tendrils, a symbol of their prayers reaching the heavens.

As the sun rose higher, the temple came alive with the sounds of clapping, chanting and ringing bells. The walls were adorned with intricate carvings, depicting scenes from Hindu mythology. The offerings, made in the form of sweets, fruits and coins at the feet of the statue of Kali, were a testament to the devotion of the pilgrims.

At the centre of the temple stood the formidable statue of Kali, her four arms raised in a menacing gesture, her tongue lolling from her open mouth. The statue was draped in garlands of flowers. The thick clouds of burning ghee from the lamps hung low in the air, filling it with its warm aroma. The sanctity of the temple was palpable, and the pilgrims bowed their heads in reverence to the divine presence that permeated the air.

For those who entered the temple, it was a place of pilgrimage, a sanctuary from the chaos of the outside world. Here, they could offer their prayers, seek blessings from the goddess and escape to a place where their voices could be heard and their wishes granted. But as the pilgrims left the temple and the sounds of the city began to filter in, a sense of foreboding lingered.

The chanting was a low rumble, punctuated by the occasional clapping and ringing of bells, echoing across the roads and into the surrounding area. The air was thick with devotion as the black statue of the Hindu goddess stood tall and imposing.

James Broun-Ramsay, the first marquess of Dalhousie and the Governor General of India, sat atop his black horse, surveying the scene before him. His hands gripped the mane tightly. A small contingent of armed riders and uniformed soldiers, brandishing swords and spears, surrounded him. His pale face with long sideburns and a neatly trimmed moustache gave him a stoic look, contrary to all the commotion around.

Ramsay had a tall figure, with a crooked posture and fair skin. His oval face was accented by piercing light green eyes, bony cheeks and a broad forehead. His black hair hung hip-length, untamed and curly. He dismounted from his horse and approached the entrance of the Kalighat Kali temple, the sounds of chanting and ringing bells growing louder. His security guard Captain Vincent Jervis stood next to him.

Dressed in his customary red coat, Ramsay cut a regal figure, exuding confidence and authority. He mounted his horse again.

'What is happening, Arpan?' Ramsay asked his orderly, who walked beside him as he rode along on his horse.

Arpan Gangopadhyay stammered, taken aback by the sudden anger in Ramsay's voice. 'A prayer, Sir.'

'Do you think I am a fool, unable to understand this pagan religion?' Ramsay's voice was sharp. 'Why is the crowd so large today?'

'Oh, no, Sir! I apologize,' Arpan replied quickly. 'Today is an important day for the temple, and devotees come from all over India to offer their prayers.'

As Ramsay's horse shifted again, the sounds of chanting and ringing bells continued, a palpable sense of devotion and reverence in the air. The Governor General was a man of power and unwavering resolve, and he would not be deterred by the chaos and mystery surrounding him.

'Special in what way?' Ramsay pressed.

'Sir,' Arpan continued, regaining his composure. 'This temple has great historical significance and it is revered by the public as one of the fifty-one Shakti Peethas.'

'The what?' Ramsay's ignorance was evident.

'I mean, my lord, it is a shrine and pilgrimage site of Shakti, the supreme goddess. It is said that the right toe of Sati fell here when Shiva was carrying her lifeless body.'

Arpan fell silent for a moment. He looked towards the temple, at the pilgrims chanting and clapping as the bells rang. The Governor General frowned and turned his head to his right. He called out to his trusted guard, Vincent. Captain Vincent Jervis was not from Scotland like the Governor General. He was an Englishman to the core and related to the royal family on his mother's side.

There was not much talking as they rode on the Grand Trunk Road. The pace was slow, and the Governor General kept his words to the minimum as he was deep in thought. After about thirty minutes, they reached the East India Company guest house. The guest house also had an office for the Governor General's use. He went about his role inside his office. He gave a few instructions to his office staff. They scrambled around without making any noise. It was going to be a long day.

The humid day turned into a relaxing evening as the winds from the Hooghly River hit the guest house. The soft breeze carried a whiff of rustic sand. There was a small gathering of four people present with the Governor General. They were having drinks, and orderlies provided the choicest cooking options, including flavours from the East, oriental dishes and Victorian styles. While the Governor General preferred whisky, the others had red wine.

Vincent was also present in the meeting. Commander Klinsmann from the British Royal Navy was a teetotaler and had a glass of *sharbat* to keep company to the senior advisors and aides of the Governor General. The latter waited for the orderlies to leave as he watched them close the wooden and brass doors. He shuffled on the sofa and leaned forward. He looked towards the group sitting in a circle and said, 'This broken region, Hindustan, is a ritualistic society, driven by blind faith.'

'Only the common people. Most of the kings, those rajas, do not care about anything but themselves,' said his red-haired security chief. Everyone looked at Captain Vincent and nodded.

'Yes, they are stooges,' continued the Governor General. 'They will not make changes and, thus, we need to make changes and bring our way of thinking and culture. Our Western thoughts will help these natives change. In time, they will adopt the Christian ways of life.'

'That is a good idea. We can be here for centuries if we bring them into our religious fold. The British Empire can rule forever with the resources present here,' said one of the advisors, who had just gulped down his fourth glass of red wine.

'Enough of the drink. You need to be sober, otherwise, you'll go to the dancer's house again and your wife will call me,' said another advisor.

The middle-aged men broke into laughter. Captain Vincent did not laugh but just cracked a smile.

'I see my good Captain is not enjoying our conversation. What happened? Did they do black magic on you, my dear Captain?' asked one of the advisors.

Captain Vincent replied with a straight face, 'They may look rustic, but in their own way, they have survived for many centuries and have their own beliefs.'

'And with these beliefs, they will continue living in the darkness,' boomed the Governor General. He stood up and slowly walked towards the open wooden windows, which were painted white. The breeze from the Hooghly was now intense, and the hair on his balding forehead flew around with the gust of air hitting him. He turned around and continued, 'My compatriots, this is what we need to change. Hindustan is our crown jewel, and we must disrupt this native culture.'

He pointed towards the advisors. 'You are right, my friends. The Western cultural influences usurping innate local culture will be the key to the British Empire's permanent stay in India. And we have seen and will continue to see more success with our Doctrine of Lapse rules.'

There was a brief chuckle, and all but one broke into laughter. Captain Vincent shook his head gently as he heard them talk about the success of the Doctrine of Lapse. He began to think. *A simple law says that any kingdom supported by the company will lose its status as a princely state if no male heir exists. They didn't want to fight us and took this route for peace. In time, many will fall.*

The company set up the Doctrine of Lapse, but the Governor General implemented it aggressively with an iron hand.

'Remember how they bring adopted sons to save their minuscule kingdoms?' said one of the advisors. They laughed again.

'Yes, again and again, we took more and more land. Satara, Udaipur...' continued one of the advisors.

'Don't forget Sambalpur,' added another.

'Yes, and we can get Jhansi next,' said the third advisor.

Vincent was snapped out of his thoughts when one of the advisor's glasses of red wine slipped from his grasp, crashing to the floor and sending the wine cascading towards the luxurious carpet in the centre of the room.

As he watched the wine spread, Vincent couldn't help but think that if the natives didn't comply, their blood might meet a similar fate. Standing up, he addressed the group, his voice ringing with authority. He warned them that their actions would only incite dissent among the rajas without them even realizing it.

The room erupted in chaos as a bottle was hurled to the ground, causing a deafening crash and spilling the last of the wine. At the sound, Arpan, who had by now reached the guest house, entered the room. His eyes widened as he took in the sight of the spilt wine. He rushed towards the table, but his movements caused another round of crashes as more glassware tumbled to the carpet. Vincent's shout echoed in the room, bringing servants running, but he quickly regained control, his voice steady as he ordered the servants to leave. The room fell silent, the only sound being that of the soft trickle of the wine.

Vincent and Klinsmann resumed their conversation, and the Governor General wasted no time in sharing his thoughts about Hindustan. 'These people are easily swayed by religion and superstition,' he declared. 'They are still living in the dark ages, with no real knowledge of science or technology.'

Vincent couldn't disagree more. 'I have met many educated

and well-read Indians,' he countered. 'They have a thirst for knowledge and a desire to learn. They are not easily manipulated.'

The Governor General scoffed at Vincent's assertion. 'You are naive,' he said. 'These people are not rational. They will always bow down to the white man.'

The group laughed, but the Governor General was not deterred. He went on to extol Britain's greatness, citing the many scholars, philosophers, scientists and poets who had emerged from their society. 'It is time for Britain to take the reins and lead the way,' he declared. 'We will create a new century for the British Empire, and the sun will never set on our reign.'

As the group continued to make a ruckus and went on with their debates, Vincent took a sip of his wine and considered the truth behind the Governor General's words. He couldn't shake the feeling that those in power were all the same, driven by megalomaniacal desires and fixated on their own notions of leadership, with little regard for the consequences of their actions outside their palaces. Vincent thought of King Henry VIII, who had a strong sense of entitlement, disregard for the consequences of his actions and desire for a male heir, which led him to break with the Catholic Church and establish the Church of England. It had far-reaching consequences for the country and its people. The Greek philosopher Plato also warned of megalomaniacal leaders in his work, *The Republic*, arguing that democracy can lead to tyranny if the wrong person is elected to lead.

Instead of dwelling further on it, Vincent decided to focus on his journey to support the army in Afghanistan and eventually return to England, where, through letters, he would share his experiences with his family, friends and especially his good friend, Charles Dickens.

Santal Parganas, 1905
Courtesy: Wikimedia Commons | https://bit.ly/3HwezqD. Accessed on 1 May 2023.

Countdown to Revolution
00:00:03

110 days before the Hul
Early morning, March 1855
Somewhere in the Santhal Land

The lake sat nestled in the heart of the dense jungle, surrounded by towering trees and thick foliage that reached up to the sky. The soft rustling of leaves and the gentle splashing of the water provided a soothing melody to the peaceful scene. A faint mist hung low over the surface of the lake, giving it an otherworldly appearance. It was a place of unspoiled beauty, untouched by the outside world, a place where time seemed to stand still. But in this idyllic setting, a warrior stood, his presence seeming to command the very earth beneath him.

Sido Murmu stood at the edge of the shimmering lake, his dark skin illuminated by the light of the rising sun. His breathing was deep, even and calm, but beneath the surface of his serenity lay a wealth of experience and scars. Each line told a story of strength, tales of surviving the strong claws of jaguars and tigers. His body was a testament to the wild—with broad hips, lean legs and feet wide enough to balance on even the most unpredictable terrain.

As the sun gently beat down on his bare chest, he raised his arms to the sky, calling out to the spirit of Marang Buru, the supreme source of power, who they worshipped in the form of nature. Sido was a warrior, a hunter, a provider, but he offered a bow of respect to the deer that had wandered into view. *Marang Buru, you watch over us,* he whispered. *Who are we in front of you? Keep guiding us and giving us strength.*

Sido closed his eyes, feeling the warmth on his eyelids from being in direct sunlight for so long. It was a luxurious experience, a moment of peace in a life full of hardships. His muscles were relaxed and firm, a result of the years he had spent working outside under harsh conditions to provide food for his family and to pay part of the produce as taxes. He stood tall, his arms spread wide, basking in the glow of the sun and the strength it provided. This was his place of power, where he communed with nature and drew strength from the spirits of the earth. He was ready to face whatever challenges lay ahead. The thirty-nine-year-old Sido, a Santhal whose ancestors had lived with nature for thousands of years, walked back from the lake towards the *kacha* trail. He followed the broken path towards the jungle and saw some wildflowers on a shrub. His face broke into a gentle smile.

Sido made his way through the lush jungle, each step a whisper on the soft forest floor. He was in his element, surrounded by the beauty that nature had to offer and that had become such a defining part of his life. For four decades, he had called this place home, each nook and cranny as familiar to him as the creases in his own skin. But today was different, something felt amiss. The air was thick with the sounds of rustling leaves and the rustle of hidden creatures. Sido could sense that there was something else at play.

As he walked, a small yet unique and sturdy red flower caught his eye. It was in a brilliant contrast against the green surroundings—its colour reminiscent of a dying flame. The five stiff yet gentle petals in the shape of a star, each with small indentations that seemed to fit perfectly into his fingers, were beginning to fade. Sido couldn't help but think of his wife, Mala, and how she would love the beauty of the flower.

Determined to find sustenance for his family, Sido set off to a new part of the jungle, his knowledge of the wilderness coming to his aid. The thick, dark forest was more than just his home, it was a part of him, a place where secrets were hidden and waiting to be discovered. As a Santhal and an adventurous seeker, Sido intimately knew the secrets that the wilderness held. He knew the surroundings like the back of his hand. But even so, he couldn't shake the feeling that someone was watching, waiting, biding their time. The jungle was alive with possibility, and Sido was ready for whatever lay ahead.

Sido walked through the fields, surrounded by the sweet fragrance of wildflowers blooming under the warm sun. He heard the melodic songs of the birds sitting on the branches above him. As he roamed through the fields, he couldn't help but smile at the sight before him. A family of ducks frolicking in the water and the peacefulness of the scene was something he wished Mala could witness. He carefully plucked a handful of delicate wildflowers and held them tenderly in his broad palm. He envisioned how much she would appreciate their beauty and the thought of her caused his heart to swell with love.

My children would also want to have a look. They must be in need of a delicious meal. Let me see if there are any fruits.

With a mission to provide his children with food, Sido set off towards the fruit trees. The honeybees buzzing around him and the busy ants on the blades of grass added to the serenity of the forest. The sight of the colourful flowers in full bloom brought to mind the idea of stability, but Sido was aware of the dangers of staying in one place for too long.

Ahh. Found you. You look ripe. Need five of you. Four for my children and the fifth for my Kanhu's son.

Sido walked across the vast fields filled with the blooming wildflowers, collecting some. As he approached a tree, he decided to sharpen the stones he carried to cut ripe fruits. His initial attempts may have missed their mark, but he was determined to succeed. With a change of strategy and a steady hand, he succeeded in collecting five fruits.

Sido held the fruits and flowers close to his chest, feeling a deep sense of gratitude for nature and acknowledging the importance of only taking what was necessary. He closed his eyes and took a moment to meditate, then opened them, and bowed with respect in front of the tree from which he had collected the fruits. With a light heart and a journey of only fifteen to twenty minutes ahead of him, Sido set off for his home, eager to share his treasures with his family.

As he walked, his mind raced with thoughts about the day ahead. The essential monthly village meeting was awaited, as the discussions would shape the future of his family and community. Their freedom to use their land and nature was at stake, and the meeting was crucial to ensure their unhindered existence.

Suddenly, a rustling of leaves interrupted his thoughts. Sido stopped in his tracks, his eyes searching the surrounding area for the source of the noise. He soon spotted a deer cautiously making its way towards him. Holding still, he watched as the deer approached, only to pause a few feet away, look at him and then wander off. Sido smiled, resumed his journey and continued his musings.

As he approached the broken path near the lake, he spotted his younger brother, Kanhu, who had come to collect freshwater fish. Kanhu was of average height with a sturdy frame and a sharp, angular face, reflecting his warrior instincts. His prominent nose, deep-set eyes and thick beard gave him a rugged appearance, and his head full of curly black hair complemented his weathered skin, scarred from years of working the fields. In spite of not being particularly muscular, Kanhu carried himself confidently.

The two brothers walked back to their hut, exchanging news and sharing stories. As they approached a small, broken-down hut, they looked at each other with a sense of anger and sadness. The hut was half-burnt, with only half a roof and two walls still standing—a sad reminder of the violence and destruction that had come to their land.

Ever since a Santhal named Bir had tried to challenge the zamindar Madho Soren a few months ago, mass gatherings had come under suspicion, but the Santhals knew it was vital for them to meet and discuss their future. Under the guise of group hunting and propitiatory rituals, the Murmu brothers gathered Santhal youths to unite and discuss their situation.

Just then, a voice broke the stillness of the air.

SIDO KANHU

'Stop, thief! Stop!'

Sido turned slowly towards the voice, a sense of unease stirring in his chest. The speaker, an agitated caretaker of the local zamindar, ran towards them, shouting.

'These trees and flowers belong to my lord, Madho Soren. You need to come with me, you fools. I will take you to my lord and he will decide what to do with both of you.'

Kanhu, with a sense of anger, tried to lunge forward, but Sido's firm grip held him back. The situation was escalating quickly, and Sido knew they needed to stay calm and think carefully about their next move. They could not afford to get captured.

110 days before the Hul
Afternoon, January 1855
Somewhere in the Santhal Land

The garden was a symphony of blooms, the air laden with the perfume of roses and Hari Champa flowers waving in the gentle breeze. Two well-dressed men stood nearby, their heads bowed in reverence as they observed the muscular figure of Madho Soren, the zamindar and moneylender who was known as the local ruler, walking among the fragrant flowers. Tension was palpable, but Madho closed his eyes, savouring the sweet scent.

Madho was a man of power and influence. His ancestral property and large landholdings granted by the East India Company officials made him an unrivalled force in the region. Through years of moneylending, he had been able to keep control over the region by putting many from the local population in debt. But in spite of his wealth and prestige, Madho found solace only in his garden, tending to the flowers as he sought to keep his mind at peace.

Footsteps approached, and a voice spoke up, 'I can see you like flowers.' It was the village *daroga* (policeman).

'They require attention and give beautiful results over time.

SIDO KANHU

It helps me keep my mind calm amidst all the challenges I've faced in the past year,' Madho replied, his eyes meeting those of the frightened policeman.

The daroga's voice trembled as he spoke, 'Yes, I understand. You're referring to the Manjhi incident from last August.'

Madho remained silent, his expression stern, his eyes betraying the pain he felt at the mention of incident. The past year had been a difficult one for him, as he had been forced to fight against those he deemed inferior. Two Santhal village chiefs, Nursingh Manjhi and Koondru Manjhi, had petitioned against the exploitation by moneylenders, like Madho, to the commissioner in Bhagalpur.

But the situation was far from simple. The Santhals had a long list of grievances, beginning with the replacement of the barter system with a cash-based economy. Unfamiliar with this new system, the simple-minded Santhals found themselves borrowing from moneylenders and repaying with sky-high interest rates, often resulting in the loss of their harvests.

The moneylenders, known as mahajans, were quick to file suits against the Santhals in court, with the latter only learning about it when a court decree would arrive, ordering the sale of their possessions, including their cattle, homes, vessels and ornaments. The Santhals would sometimes turn to their village chiefs for justice, but they would find themselves powerless, as everything was controlled by the British government.

Nursingh and Koondru's petition was a bold move, but their wait for justice was far from over. The petition had to be navigated through corrupt clerks, pleaders, peons and guards before it reached the commissioner.

The English judge had little patience for what he deemed to be 'petty' grievances as long as the revenue from farming was coming in. He was more focussed on the construction of the roads from Tinpahadia to the Rajmahal Hills, through the Damin-i-koh, an exclusive reserve for the paharias. The Santhals were employed as cultivators and day labourers, earning their survival. However, they aspired for a dignified life.

As there had been no response to the Manjhis' petition, the Santhals started protesting and voicing their concerns more vigorously than before.

Bir, a local Santhal from Lakhimpur village, had been of the view that moneylenders would go on robbing them forever. He believed that he had the law on his side if he complained and that he and other Santhals need not always be slaves to the moneylenders. However, Bir had suffered at the hands of law. Madho had sent a daroga from Burhait to punish him. The daroga, drunk on power, had showed no mercy as he physically and emotionally abused Bir and his followers, snatching their possessions and breaking their spirits.

The daroga was now waiting for his monthly bribe from Madho. Quiet descended as the Santhals reeled under the atrocities of the mahajans. While Madho was mulling over ways to retain more power, he heard footsteps and two men approached him.

'Sir, we have brought a trader who has some information about you being cheated,' they said.

Madho raised an eyebrow, intrigued. He had been expecting the arrival of his men, but he was not prepared for this unexpected news. He gestured for his two men to come closer, his eyes fixed on the stranger they had brought with them.

The trader was trembling with fear, his eyes downcast. He was well aware of the reputation of Madho Soren, a man feared and respected by many in the region.

'Speak,' Madho commanded.

The trader stammered as he began to speak, telling Madho about a group of Santhals who had been cheating him out of his fair share of profits from their ventures in the jungle. The man's words were filled with urgency as if he feared for his life.

Madho listened intently, his mind racing. He had built his empire on trust and loyalty, and he would not tolerate anyone threatening it.

As the trader finished speaking, Madho stood up, his towering presence intimidating the two men and the Santhal. He strode towards his two henchmen, his eyes blazing with anger. 'Gather my men. It is time to teach these Santhals a lesson. Start collecting the outstanding money they owe us,' he growled, his voice filled with determination.

The two men nodded, afraid to say a word. They quickly disappeared, leaving Madho and the daroga alone in the garden.

'You're not planning on handling this on your own, are you?' the daroga asked, his voice filled with concern.

Madho turned to him, his eyes cold and calculating. 'I have built this empire on my own, and I will not hesitate to protect it.' With that, he turned and walked away, his mind already set on his mission. The daroga watched him go, knowing that the coming days would be filled with danger and uncertainty.

But Madho was not afraid. He had faced challenges before, and he would face them again. For him, it was just another opportunity to prove his strength and power.

The night was dark and the air was thick with the sweet aroma of Hari Champa as Madho made his way to the place where his men were waiting. He was going to unleash terror to remind everyone who was the powerful one. He was Madho Soren, the powerful zamindar and moneylender, and he was not one to be trifled with. He would give out loans, take their thumbprints on paper without giving them the full picture of what they were getting themselves into and then take their land and force them to work as labourers. The British law, designed to reinforce the power of those in power, was definitely not on the Santhals' side.

91 days before the Hul
Evening, March 1855
Somewhere in the Santhal Land

In the small village nestled amidst the rolling hills, there stood a hut unlike any other. Though its walls were made of humble bamboo sticks and mud, it was a place of warmth and love, where the sound of laughter and the aroma of cooking filled the air. This was the home of Sido and his wife, Mala.

A few days had passed since the flower-plucking incident, but the false peace continued to linger. Sido knew that Madho and the daroga were dangerous enemies, and he had to find a way to negotiate with Madho Soren's Tinpahadia jungle caretaker to avoid any conflict.

Kanhu was initially angry and reluctant to go, but Sido managed to calm him down. He explained that they had to speak to the caretaker or Madho might misunderstand and send men or a daroga to their village to cause trouble.

In spite of his initial hesitation, Kanhu trusted his elder brother and went along with the plan. As Sido spoke softly to the caretaker, Kanhu watched in awe. At first, the caretaker was unyielding, but Sido's calm demeanour and gentle persuasion eventually won him over. The caretaker promised not to report the visit to Madho and even agreed to blame any damage in the area on the deer.

Sido thanked the caretaker and offered Kanhu's assistance if needed. The younger brother was full of admiration for Sido's negotiation skills, knowing that he was a peacemaker at heart, not a coward.

As the sun began its slow descent towards the horizon, Sido made his way back to the hut, tired but content after a day's toil in the fields. He found Mala waiting for him, her beauty a beacon that illuminated the simple space.

'Welcome back,' she said, her smile lighting up her face. 'I was getting worried.'

Sido returned her smile, feeling a warm glow in his chest. He washed his hands with water in the bucket kept at the entrance and took his place on the ground beside her.

'I'm fine,' he replied. 'Have the kids eaten?'

The couple ate their dinner in companionable silence, savouring each bite and the comfort of each other's company. After they finished, Sido went to check on their children, who were sleeping soundly in the next room. Their family was a source of pride and joy, with three sons and two daughters, all aged between two and fourteen. Their eldest son worked outside the village and their eldest daughter had got married the previous year.

As the night grew darker, the chirping of the birds outside grew louder. Mala rose from her seat and walked to the window, from where she watched the birds return to their nests. This was a ritual she performed every evening, but tonight, as she gazed out into the night, she felt a pang of sadness. Sido noticed and approached her, taking her hands in his.

'What's bothering you?' he asked, concern etched on his face.

'I was just thinking about whether we will ever be happy and free like the birds,' she replied, her voice soft. 'Being free from the constant worry of having our hard-earned money taken away by the *diku*s (moneylenders). Imagine a life with no debt, no dikus, just us and nature. That would be true happiness.'

Sido felt a pang in his chest, knowing exactly what she meant. The dikus were a constant source of fear and anxiety in their lives. They preyed on their vulnerabilities, offering credit at exorbitant interest rates. It was a vicious cycle that kept them trapped in a web of debt, with no escape in sight. Sido had seen friends and neighbours lose their land and homes to the dikus, their dreams shattered in an instant. The fear of being next in line hung heavy over them, like a dark cloud that never dissipates. In spite of their hard work and determination, they were always one bad harvest away from ruin.

Sido was quiet for a moment, lost in thought, as he considered Mala's words. He nodded, patted her shoulder and embraced her.

A single tear trickled down her cheek. 'I wish we could be free from the dikus, free from the burden of debt and interest. I wish we could live a simple life, being free, surrounded by the beauty of nature.'

He watched Mala gaze out the window, the gentle breeze blowing and the faint moonlight casting shadows on the trees. He sighed heavily.

88 days before the Hul
Little after dusk, April 1855
Near Murshidabad

Major Vincent Jervis was a man of contradictions. He was proud of his family's long military tradition but conflicted about his role as a soldier. The Grenadier Guards unit of the British Army was in his blood—his ancestors had served in the regiment since its formation centuries ago. Yet, he was haunted by his actions in the line of duty.

Vincent found solace in his passion for painting and drawing. It was during one of these creative pursuits in the jungle that he had helped and saved the life a local Santhal. During this encounter, he had met Mina, who was the granddaughter of the Santhal. He had been struck by her beauty. Her features were a stark contrast to the women he had encountered in his life, and he had found himself drawn to her despite his obligations back in England.

He had struggled with his feelings, torn between his sense of duty and the sin of desire.

Vincent stood before the mirror, examining his reflection. He was a tall, muscular and well-built man, with short blonde hair, heavy-lidded green eyes, a triangular face and a pointed nose.

His skin was pale, with a hint of sunburn from his time on the subcontinent. A scar, a reminder of his time in Afghanistan, was visible on his cheek.

Vincent left the bedroom and went to his study, where the lamp was still burning. He sat at his desk and pulled out an envelope, ready to pen a letter to his dear friend Dickens. But as he began to write, his mind drifted back to Mina, her beauty and the dilemma he faced. This place was better than Afghanistan, he thought. Lucknow was good and Murshidabad was better, but here, he had something to look forward to. The thought filled him with both excitement and fear as he wondered what the future held.

15 May 1855

My dearest friend Charles,

I trust this letter finds you in good health and high spirits, and that your work on *Little Dorrit* is progressing to your satisfaction. It was with great delight that I was able to peruse a few pages of the manuscript you so kindly shared with me, and I do hope that the final draft will be completed in the near future.

Pray forgive me for not having written sooner, for I was engaged in travel. I bid farewell to Afghanistan and am now stationed in Hindustan. My transfer first took me to Lucknow, where I tarried for three months, before making my way to Calcutta. This city is home to a substantial European population, made up mainly of Christian missionaries, and I am thoroughly enjoying the company of its residents.

At present, I am making my way from Calcutta to Murshidabad and the surrounding jungles, which is proving to be quite an adventure. I have heard that the Santhals are encamped but a few leagues from the town, and I am eager to make their acquaintance. The heat is indeed oppressive, but I have found much to admire in this exotic land. Last week, I had the pleasure of driving a herd of magnificent elephants about the gardens of the Nawab of Murshidabad's residence. One of the beasts weighed no less than 20 tonnes, while another was a massive bull, over 12 feet in height and weighing nearly 1,600 kg. Such creatures are truly awe-inspiring!

I am hopeful that I shall return to Britain early next year, and I may have some good news to share with you then. More on that at a later date. I must be off soon, and I hope to make my way back to Bombay by November, to catch a ship home. Should I miss the steamer, I have made alternative arrangements to return as soon as possible. I then plan to make arrangements for my return to Hindustan.

I must ask a favour of you, my friend. I do hope to hear from you before I set sail, and if for any reason you are unable to assist me, I would be most grateful if Mrs Dickens could offer her aid. I trust that all is well since I left London and that there has been no escalation in tensions between Russia and Turkey. My friend Sir Henry Brougham informed me that relations between the two countries remain cordial, and I do hope he is correct.

Yours ever faithfully,
Vincent

SIDO KANHU

There was nothing else he could say to his good friend who lived near his hometown in England. He folded the thin white paper and placed it inside a sealed envelope addressed to his fiancée Helena Gerome. She would give the letter to Charles.

I am committing a sin thinking about Mina.

It was time to go back to bed. He had to wake up early. But all he did was toss and turn, thinking of Mina.

85 days before the Hul
Before evening, April 1855
Bhognadih

In the heart of Bhognadih village, the Santhals were gathering to celebrate the Sarhul festival, a time of optimism and gratitude in an otherwise harsh world. For many, the past year had been one of great hardship, with the power of the East India Company and the zamindars leaving them to struggle. Chunar, a Santhal, had lost both his ancestral home and land to the zamindars, a tragedy that had resulted in his family taking their lives by jumping into the river during the monsoon season.

But for now, the Santhals were focussing on the present, on the joy of the festival and the hope for a better future. The houses in the village were decorated modestly, but the festive fervour was palpable.

One of the key rituals of the Sarhul festival was the worship of a sacred Sal tree every year, selected by the village elders and decorated with colourful flags, flowers and other offerings. The tree was believed to be the symbol of Dharti Mata, or Goddess Earth, and was worshipped during the festival as a way to seek her blessings for a good harvest and prosperity.

As the sun began to set on the village, casting a warm glow

over the streams that flowed through its heart, Mala and Sido sat by the water's edge, their legs dangling in the cool water. Mala leaned her head on Sido's shoulder, lost in thought. But Sido noticed that something was troubling her. There was a hint of sadness in her eyes.

With concern etched on his face, he gently lifted her chin and asked, 'Is everything alright? I can see that you're not as excited about today as you should be.'

Mala sighed, her gaze softening as she replied, 'I'm not upset, Sido. I'm just worried about you.'

Sido's brows furrowed in confusion. 'About me? What could you possibly have to worry about when I'm right here with you?' he asked, taking her hands in his own.

'I had a dream,' Mala said, her voice low and serious.

Sido tried to lighten the mood, and jokingly said, 'Well, let's hope it wasn't about having more kids!'

Mala smiled, but it didn't reach her eyes. 'No, not at all.'

'Well, was it about me sitting on the throne, with you by my side, wearing a crown on your head?' Sido asked, a playful grin on his face.

Mala smiled a little more, caught up in the made-up story, adding to it, 'Yes, exactly. You were sitting on the throne, with me by your side, and I could see a crown on my head,' she said, her voice filled with amusement.

As Sido held Mala's hand, he chuckled and drew her nearer, his grip tightening. 'Indeed, that is not a bad dream. I promise to always stand by you, no matter the circumstance,' he said with a reassuring smile. 'You needn't worry. The Sarhul festival serves as a reminder that we are never alone in this world. We have the support of our community, each other and the blessings of Dharti Mata. Together, we shall confront any adversity that arises, with optimism and hope filling our hearts.'

Just then, a friend of Sido called out to him from a distance, pulling him away to attend the festivities. Mala watched as Sido walked away, surrounded by friends and family.

As the evening turned to night, the village came alive with the sounds of festivities. It was a special day for cattle, as the deity of animals, Lord Pashupati, was also worshipped on the day. Cows were bathed, massaged and adorned with vermillion.

By evening, they all gathered for prayers and the lighting of diyas. A modest feast was held to break the fast later in the day.

The festivities continued throughout the night, with the villagers gathering around the temple to sing praises of the gods and express their gratitude for another year of survival. The young men played musical instruments while others danced merrily; offerings of rice, ghee and sugarcane juice accompanied by sweetened milk were given to the deities.

Sido saw Harivan, a senior Santhal who was over sixty years old, and bowed to him, conveying his respect. Harivan, in turn, bowed back, a reminder of the bond they had formed a few months prior when Sido and Vincent had saved Harivan's life.

As Harivan had trudged through the dense jungle that fateful day, he had felt the weight of despair crushing him. He had come to the jungle to end his life, unable to bear the loneliness and hopelessness that was consuming him—his crops had failed and he found himself unable to take care of his grandchild. But as he prepared the noose to take his final breath, a British officer named Vincent Jervis had appeared on the scene, shouting and startling Harivan. The sudden disturbance had caused Harivan to jump, but Vincent had carried him to safety.

In spite of Harivan's protests and pleas to be left alone, Vincent had held on firmly, determined to save the man's life. The commotion had drawn Sido's attention, who was fishing near the lake at the time. At first, he had thought that Vincent was attacking Harivan, but upon closer inspection, he had realized that it was not so.

Sido spoke the local language, and with Vincent's broken words, the two men had fortunately been able to communicate. Sido had to climb the tree and use a sharp-edged stone to cut the rope, saving Harivan from suffocating to death. The two men had spoken with Harivan, with Sido offering help and Vincent explaining the importance of respecting life and the principles of God. As the three men had made their way back to Sido's village, Vincent had explained that he was a Major in the British Army, seeking escape from the reality of his life for a few days, and also said that he painted to remain in touch with nature.

In Sido's village, Harivan and his granddaughter, Mina, had received a warm welcome with open arms, and Vincent had joined them for the evening meal. The meal had been a simple affair. After the meal, Sido had offered them a small cup of sweetened milk—it was considered lucky if one could finish the contents of the cup without spilling a single drop.

As in the present, the family gathered for their evening prayers and for the exchange of pleasantries. They shared the good things in their lives and emphasized the importance of each member in the community. The children could be seen playing games and running around, enjoying the festival. They felt a deep sense of connection to their community and to their culture, and they knew that Sarhul was a time to celebrate both.

As the festival came to an end, Sido's family felt a sense of sadness but also gratitude. They were grateful for their community, for their culture and for each other. They knew that they may not have much, but they had each other and that was enough.

85 days before the Hul
Sometime in the night, April 1855
British Barracks, 20 km east of Bhognadih

The gust of wind howled through the night, causing the windows to rattle and bang like ghostly whispers. The officers spoke about their views on Santhals and their experiences of their encounters. Soon, it was Vincent's turn. He described how he had saved Harivan's life, and the other officers listened with mixed reactions.

'You shouldn't have intervened,' one of them said, his voice dripping with contempt.

'It is not an honourable death. No one should die like that,' Vincent countered, his gaze stern.

'They're just vessels of labour for us,' another officer interjected. 'These tribals don't understand honour.'

Vincent shook his head in disagreement, his voice rising with conviction. 'God gave us life and we must protect it. Remember, Exodus 20:13. Suicide is murder, and the sixth commandment says, "Thou shall not kill."'

As he spoke, a voice interrupted from the door, 'Attention everyone, CO in the room.'

The commanding officer of the regiment, General Edmund

Rowlands, entered the room and took stock of the situation. 'I heard the discussion,' he began, his tone authoritative. 'I don't want any more of these petty issues. These tribals must be shown their place. We're here for the Empire and what we can gain from these lands. We're here to win this land. Are there any questions?'

Everyone in the room fell silent, and General Rowlands continued, 'Very well. Now, I will speak to Major Vincent.' Vincent stood at attention, saluted and followed his superior out of the room.

Once alone, General Rowlands turned to Vincent. 'So, you didn't allow the man to die,' he said, his tone curious.

'No Sir, I couldn't let him die,' Vincent replied, his voice resolute.

'Do you think he might have died if you had let him?' General Rowlands asked, his gaze piercing.

'Yes Sir, I know he would have died,' Vincent replied in a firm voice. 'But it wouldn't have been an honourable death, it would have been cowardice.'

The General listened intently as Vincent recounted the details of his experience, including Harivan and Mina's journey to Sido's village.

'Do you believe that suicide is a sin and not honourable because of the Bible?' General Rowlands asked in an analytical tone.

Vincent looked around the room, taking in the presence of his senior officer and a few orderlies. He nodded, speaking with conviction about his beliefs.

General Rowlands gave a gentle smile, and his tone softened,

'And who is Mina? Is she someone special?'

Vincent blushed, and the General could see a spark in his eyes as they talked about Mina.

'She is the same person,' Vincent said in a hushed voice.

'Who?' General Edmund asked, his brow furrowing.

'The tigress,' Vincent replied with a hint of pride in his voice.

'Oh, so you found her?' General Edmund was turning curious.

'Yes, I found her,' Vincent said, his gaze steady.

Vincent had met Mina briefly a month before Harivan's incident. He had been in the forest painting when he had heard a commotion. Going closer to the source of the noise, he had seen two bandits attacking a group of Santhal womenfolk. It was there that he had come across Mina, who had been busy fighting back. He had then jumped in to save the women—the bandits had been overpowered one by one by Mina and Vincent. Together, they had managed to capture one bandit while the rest ran away. As Vincent had been tying up the bandit with his belt, Mina and the other women had left. But he had noticed her looking at him from afar.

'You should give her a gift,' General Edmund suggested, a sly smile playing on his lips as he noticed Vincent's expression softening.

Vincent suddenly became a little uncomfortable. Before he could react, the topic of their discussion shifted abruptly as the General turned to a more pressing concern—the recent raids by marauders on local moneylenders. Vincent listened attentively as his superior outlined the plan to counter these attacks and maintain peace in the colony.

When their discussion concluded, the General dismissed Vincent and the latter retired to his quarters. As he lay on his bed, thoughts about Mina filled his mind. Her petite form, brown skin and captivating gaze had consumed his thoughts for several nights now. In spite of his attempts to shake her out of his mind, her smile, her beautiful face, her delicate features stayed with him—a persistent reminder of the spark of infatuation that had taken hold of his heart.

As he lay in the stillness of his quarters, Vincent pondered over the confusion that filled his heart. Was this mere infatuation or something deeper? The night drifted as Vincent struggled with these thoughts, the wind howling outside as if in sympathy with the turmoil within him.

84 days before the Hul
Late night, April 1855
Jungles of the Santhal Land

Vincent was dressed in his uniform. He had tied his horse to a nearby tree. The majestic creature was eating grass and moving its hooves gently on the ground as it grazed. Vincent leaned his back on the mossy tree bark, one hand on his hips and the other hand swinging a stick he found nearby. He scanned his eyes and saw someone familiar coming towards him.

Mina.

She was wearing a green-and-brown saree and was taking small steps towards him. Her long, black hair was glistening in the moonlight. Her ankle bracelet was making a gentle, sweet sound from a distance. Her earrings were moving with every step she took. Her bindi was placed perfectly in the centre of her forehead, and the three dots in the centre of her chin couldn't be missed.

Couldn't have seen more beautiful hair ever! Vincent said to himself.

Mina had no idea she possessed such power over him. She looked at Vincent closely as she walked close to him. She was also attracted to him.

He extended his right arm as she came close to him, and

he took a few steps ahead once she stopped. They stared at each other for a moment without uttering any word. There was something they both felt instinctively when looking into each other's eyes. They seemed connected even if their life and culture were miles apart.

'Mina!' His voice called out her name.

Her face turned towards him at the sound of his deep baritone. She smiled as she looked up at him. Her heart beat faster each time he called her name. Her body quivered under the pleasure caused by him calling out her name.

'I'm here, Major,' she answered sweetly in her soft voice.

'I did not expect you to come,' said Vincent, looking at her feet. She was barefoot. As she bent forward, so did his eyes. She didn't speak, but certain gestures shared what words could not.

'I did not know I would come,' she replied.

The night air was crisp, with the occasional gust of wind blowing as Mina and Vincent stood together, lost in their own thoughts. Mina was resting her head on Vincent's broad chest, and she could hear his increasing heartbeat. She was comforted by the warmth of his embrace and the familiarity of his scent.

Vincent was captivated by Mina's beauty, her fearless personality and her love for nature. Her innocence and aura also charmed him.

In the light of the moon, Vincent could see her well. He saw the thin cut above her left eyebrow, a souvenir from the recent fight with bandits, and the faint scar by the corner of her lips that made her look mysterious. Mina's presence was alluring, and Vincent felt the urge to know everything about her.

'What do we do next?' Mina asked, breaking the silence between them. She could sense the tension and the unspoken words that lingered in the air.

'Let's talk,' Vincent replied. 'I want to tell you about myself, but first I need to know more about you.' Mina looked into his eyes intently, but she didn't say anything.

Vincent had Mina close to him, and moved his lips close to hers. She was nervous, trying to hold on to him. He was lost in her warm gaze.

Suddenly, Vincent's horse neighed and shook its head, breaking the silence of the night. 'We can't stay here,' Vincent whispered. 'Someone might come.' He placed a hand on Mina's shoulder and gently urged her towards the horse. He then mounted the saddle and looked back at Mina. The moon shone on her face, giving her an angelic appearance. Mina climbed up behind Vincent and held on to him tightly.

I will bring the Lord into our talk soon. Mina needs to see the power of Christ.

Vincent was a man of faith, a devout Christian, and he longed to share his beliefs with Mina. But she seemed to dodge the topic, evading his questions and changing the subject. He couldn't understand why she was so reluctant to discuss religion, especially when he could see how much good it brought into his life.

As they rode over the rugged terrain, Vincent once again tried to broach the topic. 'Mina, have you ever considered the teachings of Jesus Christ?' he asked, his voice soft and sincere.

Mina tensed up, her grip on Vincent's waist tightening. *Why he is bringing up this topic? Why does he want me to change?* she thought. 'Can we not talk about this right now?' she replied, her voice filled with apprehension.

Vincent could sense her discomfort, and he didn't want to push her too hard. He was patient and understanding, always respecting her wishes. 'Of course, my dear. We can discuss it another time,' he said, placing a gentle kiss on her hand. But he was determined to find a way to convince Mina about the superiority of his faith, and he couldn't help but wonder why she was so hesitant. He was confident that once she saw the peace and comfort that came with embracing Christianity, she would be eager to join him on this spiritual journey.

As they continued on, Vincent couldn't shake the feeling that something was holding Mina back from exploring his religion. He was determined to uncover the truth and help her find the path to enlightenment. He started talking on the topic again.

'Take me back now.'

'But we have more time.'

'Take me back now!'

Vincent was taken aback when he saw the expression on Mina's face. She looked like she was about to cry. 'Are you sure?' he asked, stroking her hair. 'I'll protect you.'

Mina smiled and nodded, 'You have my trust,' she said. 'We fought together against the bandits, and I couldn't have made it without you.'

Vincent placed a gentle kiss on Mina's hand and started to guide the horse forward, navigating through the rocky and uneven terrain, taking her back towards her village. Mina clung to him.

In spite of Mina's reticence, Vincent remained optimistic. He was deeply in love with her, and he wanted to share everything with her, including his faith. He was determined to convert her, not through force or coercion, but through love and understanding.

~

84 days before the Hul
Early morning, April 1855
Jungles of the Santhal Land

Sido and his youngest son's footsteps were silent as they trudged through the dense mist that clung to the jungle floor. The wind whistled through the tall grass, a ghostly chorus that echoed through the trees. In the pre-dawn light, the two of them were a single entity, their movements in perfect unison as they journeyed deeper into the heart of the jungle.

He came to a stop at the base of a towering Sal tree—its trunk large and rough, its branches alive with the chirping of birds. Sido moved his hand across the trunk, feeling the ridges, the insects crawling across its bark. He stooped, picking up a broken piece of a stone, feeling its warm surface in his hand. The place where they had reached held great significance for Sido. This was the place where he used to spend countless hours with his father.

'It was not so very long ago,' he whispered, lost in thought as memories came flooding back to him. He remembered the day his father died and how he had bitterly cried for days. His father had told him before his demise that death was not the end but a chance to become part of nature. But that could not console Sido, who still missed him deeply.

With a final kiss to the stone, Sido rose and stepped into a clearing. In the centre of the clearing was a shallow hole surrounded by tall piles of stones. In the centre of the hole was a flat rock, smooth to the touch. Sido reached for his pouch and retrieved a small knife. He kneeled before the rock. It was large, but not too heavy for him to lift. Using the blade of the knife, he carefully scraped away the dirt from its surface.

As he lifted the rock to clean it, Sido's heart swelled with emotion. It had been many years since he had last visited this place, but the memories were still fresh in his mind. He knelt down and murmured as if talking softly to the ground, speaking about the changes that had taken place in their village, about the new people who had come to live there and about the festivals they had celebrated over the years. Sido explained to his son that this was the place where his father had brought him to explain the connection Santhals have with nature. With a final kiss to the Sal tree leaves, he carefully placed the rock from where he had picked it up and arranged some dry leaves around it.

Sido stepped out of the clearing and smiled at his son. He said, 'Come, we must walk down this path.' The two of them set off towards the riverbank, the cool morning air filling their lungs with the fresh scent of the impending rain. As they walked, Sido spoke to his son about the importance of water and rivers, likening them to the blood that coursed through their veins.

As the young boy dipped his hand playfully in the stream, he listened intently to the wise words of his father. 'The river gives life to the ground,' his father said, reminding him of the delicate balance that existed in nature. They walked back to the tree, and the boy noticed smoke rising from the dry leaves placed around the rock.

'Father, smoke!' he said, pointing towards it.

Sido smiled at his son's attentiveness and asked, 'So, son, where there is smoke, there is...?'

Having understood, the boy replied, 'Fire.' A smile appeared on his face as he realized the importance of this lesson. As he looked at the flames of the fire, he became concerned. 'The fire can spread, father,' he said worriedly.

Sido questioned him, 'Can it?'

The young boy thought for a moment before answering, 'They are stones. Stones do not burn.' His father smiled, appreciating his son's quick thinking.

Sido paused, looking into his son's eyes, 'You must be like stone sometimes. In spite of all the pain and suffering around, you need not burn all your emotions but learn to control yourself. Do not lose your temper. You must show patience, no matter what happens. Be strong and you will succeed,' he said.

The boy turned to leave, but then stopped and looked back at his father. 'Father?' he asked.

'Yes?' Sido replied.

'Thank you,' the boy said with gratitude. Sido's eyes moistened as he embraced his son. It was a moment of pure love and bonding between the father–son duo.

As they stood in silence, they could hear the jungle come alive. But suddenly, a thumping, the sound of galloping caught Sido's attention.

77 days before the Hul
Afternoon, April 1855
Bhagalpur

Commissioner G.F. Brown sat back in his chair, his frown deepening. Major Vincent took another sip of his tea, savouring the warmth and the seemingly bitter taste of the drink. He watched the steam rising from the cup, forming little clouds that drifted towards the open window. He could feel the tension in the room, the unspoken words, the unsaid doubts. He waited patiently, knowing that the commissioner needed time to process what he had said.

Finally, Brown spoke, his voice low and hesitant, 'I see your point, Major. But we cannot just let them live in their primitive ways, can we? We must civilize them to bring them into the modern world. That's what our empire is built on, isn't it?' Brown asked, his question mostly rhetorical.

'I would agree with you,' replied Vincent. 'Religion plays a significant role in the lives of these people, but the way they worship is different.'

'What do you mean?' Brown asked.

'It is about the nature of Santhal worship,' explained Vincent. 'Santhal mythology shows evidence that all religions are associated with nature.' He added, pointing to a small hillock nearby, 'There stands a shrine that contains the images of their deity known as Marang Buru or Thakur. They are all pagan and need to be shown the light. That is why I am bringing in our missionaries who have done a great job in Africa.'

The world has much to learn from the people hidden deep down in those hills! But we also have a moral obligation to educate them in civilized ways, Vincent thought to himself.

Brown took a couple of sips of his tea again and continued, 'We call ourselves modern and progressive and believe in science, reason and logic. But these people believe in superstition, blind faith and idolatry. Should we not change them?'

'That is a good and difficult question,' replied Vincent.

'And the answer is simple,' Brown said, smiling. 'That's why you want to bring our Christian missionaries here. It's a noble idea, and it is God's way.'

'I am not a supporter of control,' replied Vincent. 'It's their land, and we can live in harmony. They can pay their taxes. What I am more concerned about is providing them with the direction of the light of Jesus and spreading love.'

Brown laughed loudly. 'But how does that work out practically?' he asked, raising his eyebrows and looking straight into Vincent's eyes.

'Practically, there should be some order first,' Vincent calmly explained. 'You see, Sir, they have no written scripture or organized priesthood. Their whole society lives by custom and tradition, and each village has its own customs and religious beliefs, which have been passed down through generations. If this goes unchecked, there can be no progress because each generation follows what is passed down to them. Therefore, there is no room for change and they remain the same.'

'You mean they remain savages.'

'No, Sir. They live in harmony and in groups like us, and have rules.'

Brown's frown deepened as he watched Vincent pause to catch his breath and sip his hot tea. When Vincent finally spoke, his voice was solemn. 'They have a system of balance with nature,' he said.

Brown shook his head, his eyes narrowing. 'You seem to be sympathetic towards them. Is it because of the native girl you keep meeting?' he asked.

Vincent leaned back in his chair, his expression changing as he realized that Brown knew about Mina. He remained silent for a moment, and the two men kept staring at each other. Both men were thoughtful, but for different reasons.

'Do you really think you can hide something like this?' Brown asked in a firm tone. 'Why do you think I called you here?'

Vincent understood. His senior officers wanted to use him to extract information about the tribe. He tried to speak, but words got stuck in his throat. He tried to maintain his composure, though he felt angry at being used this way.

'Sir, I hope my views are clear,' Vincent said softly, almost pleading.

The conversation shifted to another topic then.

As Vincent rose to leave, he heard Brown's parting words: 'You must try to convert the tribals instead of preaching the gospel to others. You must do as commanded.'

Vincent stood at attention, his tone severe, 'It will not be easy, Sir.'

'We are the British Empire,' Brown replied. 'We don't do easy things.'

'Their leaders will not allow it,' Vincent said. 'It may not be easy to convince them and it will take time.'

'Then we take out the leaders.'

Vincent felt a sudden unease, his stomach churning and his throat tightening. He didn't flinch, not wanting to show his reaction. 'What do you mean?' he asked, confused. 'Targeted assassination?'

Brown walked towards Vincent, looking him straight in the eyes. 'No,' he whispered. 'We create an atmosphere that will give us a reason to attack them. Then we take them out. And I know how to do it.'

The air grew thick with tension as the sound of the ticking of the clock filled the room. Vincent saluted and left. He was feeling disturbed. He knew that Brown's plan was not something he could support, but he also knew that the Empire's demands were not to be taken lightly. He had a difficult choice to make and the consequences would be dire.

Countdown to Revolution
00:00:02

69 days before the Hul
Early morning, April 1855
Bhognadih

Sido watched as his wife meticulously arranged the fruits in front of Thakur's mud idol, her hands moving gracefully as she prayed. The sunlight filtered through the trees, casting a golden glow on her face. Mala's smile was radiant as she finished her prayers, and Sido couldn't help but feel his heart swell with love for his wife.

After leaving a few fruits near the idol, Mala stepped outside their hut and began to distribute the rest of the fruits to their neighbours. Sido watched as she moved with effortless grace, her laughter ringing through the air as she chatted with the other women. He couldn't help but feel a deep sense of pride.

As the sun began to set behind the hills, Sido's family gathered around the fire in their hut. They shared stories of their day, and Sido's mother started preparing for dinner. Sido's youngest son sat close to the fire, his eyes fixed on the dancing flames.

'It's magical,' the little boy exclaimed, his voice full of wonder. 'I'm sure there is magic in this fire. It dances to its own tune and seems to be alive with its flickering light.'

Sido and Mala exchanged a glance, admiring their son's

fascination with fire. But as the boy continued to stare at the fire, they began to sense a strange energy emanating from it.

'The fire doesn't want me to come close to it,' the boy whispered, his eyes wide with awe.

Mala's smile faded, but she soon smiled again. 'Do you want to see how magic works?' she asked their son, trying to mask the fear in her voice.

The boy nodded eagerly, and Mala began to chant a simple incantation, her voice low and melodic. She then began fanning the fire. The air grew thick with tension as the flames grew higher and higher and then started to die down.

Mala took two thick pieces of wood and arranged them neatly on either side of the fire. The crackling sound of burning logs filled the room as she slowly moved them closer until they touched. The children watched her in awe as she removed her hand. A spark flew across the logs, leaving behind a small flame. 'My children, this is how fire can be controlled,' Mala said with a smile, as the flames flickered and danced.

The elder son in the room, with a look of wonder on his face, spoke up, 'Maa, I want to say something.'

'Of course, my dear,' Mala replied.

'This fire can change anything, from stone to metal, even water. Our emotions too are like fire,' he said in a wise tone. His mother nodded, pleased with his insight.

'But this fire in front of you, if misused, will destroy everything. We must be cautious before using or handling it. When mishandled, it becomes dangerous and destroys everything,' Mala warned, patting him on the head and giving him a gentle embrace.

The youngest son, his eyes shining bright, came forward and knelt before the fire, folding his hands in prayer. The whole family followed his lead, as they all prayed to the dancing flames.

As the evening turned into night, Sido lit the lamps, and they all sat together in the centre of the hut. The youngest son, lost in thought, was asked by his father, 'What are you thinking about, son?'

'Nothing much,' the child replied, but then added, 'I was thinking about the fire.'

'Fire is important,' Sido said. 'We couldn't live without it. It gives us the energy to survive, just like the sun.'

He nodded, 'And Thakur gave us the fruits, to give us strength to fight those who bring pain to his believers.'

Sido held his youngest son tightly and gently kissed his forehead, 'You are right, my son. We must be strong and fight for what we believe in.'

As they sat around a lamp, the room was filled with the soft glow of its light, and the gentle sound of the family's conversation and laughter. Little did they know that the night was far from over and that the dangers lurking in the darkness would soon find their way to their doorstep.

Is Thakur talking through him? Do we need to fight back against these mahajans and the British? Sido thought.

As Sido sat quietly outside his hut, his mind was filled with uncertainty. He recalled the story his mother had told him about fighting back when faced with danger. But this was no ordinary threat. The mahajans and the British were powerful, and he wasn't sure if he was capable of taking them on.

He looked around at the village. The lit lamps all across the village had brought a sense of calm and togetherness. But he couldn't shake the feeling that there was danger lurking in the shadows.

Sido's thoughts turned to Thakur and the words his youngest son had spoken earlier. Was it really God speaking through him? Did Thakur want them to fight back against the oppressors? Sido couldn't be sure, but he knew that he couldn't simply ignore the possibility.

The moon rose high in the sky. As the light cast soft shadows across the ground, Sido walked back towards his hut. The silence was deafening and his thoughts were continuing to swirl in his head. He wondered if he was worthy of the task that lay before him. Could he really stand up to the mahajans and the British? The thought of having to choose between fighting and dying sent shivers down his spine.

But as he went inside his hut, a sense of peace washed over him. The gentle light of the moon, coming through his window, seemed to bring to him some calm.

Sido understood that he had a difficult road ahead of him, and he also knew that he couldn't give up. He had to find a way to fight back against the evil moneylenders who threatened his village and his people. And with that determination in his heart, he closed his eyes and went to sleep.

49 days before the Hul
Early morning, May 1855
Bhognadih

It was early morning, and the Santhals huddled outside Sido's hut, an air of desperation clinging to them like the morning dew. One man was sobbing uncontrollably, tears streaming down his cheeks and the others were desperately trying to calm him, but to no avail. The sound of the sobbing man was a mournful dirge to their troubles.

Suddenly, the door of the hut creaked open and a figure stepped out. Kanhu, Sido's younger brother—his beard heavy and unkempt, his moustache a wild, tangled mess—appeared like an avenging angel, a glimmer of hope in the darkness.

'What's all this?' he asked, his voice ringing out like a clarion call. 'Has someone died?'

The four men looked at each other, and one stepped forward, his hair tied in three braids, a symbol of his station. 'Sido?' he asked hesitantly.

'No,' Kanhu replied, his voice tinged with concern. 'I am Kanhu. Sido is my elder brother. He has just gone to attend to some chores.'

The men explained their predicament of how Madho Soren

and his men had taken their land and their two children into custody, how today was the last day to pay the ransom or their land would be taken and their children would be lost forever.

Kanhu listened, his eyes widening with anger, his mind racing with thoughts of the heartless moneylender who was exploiting his tribesmen. He clenched his fists, and a fire burned in his eyes, a fierce determination to protect his people.

He stood at the threshold of the hut, his eyes scanning the room, a place filled with memories of his childhood and of the days when he had lain curled against the wall, exhausted from play. He reached for the large wooden box, and his sister-in-law, Mala, appeared, her eyes widening in surprise as she saw him take out a sword.

'Will you not wait for your brother?' she asked, her voice trembling with fear.

'Time is of essence,' Kanhu replied in a firm and unwavering voice. 'We are Santhals, and we need to protect our brothers.'

Mala knew better than to argue with him or to try to reason with the impulsive young man who would not listen. She watched him go—a solitary figure walking into the darkness of the unknown future, his sword a symbol of the courage and determination that burned in his heart. This was a man who would stop at nothing to protect his people, and at that moment, she knew that the future of the Santhals was in good hands.

Meanwhile, Sido stood by the stream, feeling refreshed after his bath. He was ready to tackle whatever the day had in store for him. As he made his way back to the village, he noticed that something was amiss. The usually bustling hamlet was now eerily quiet, with clusters of people huddled together in hushed whispers. Mala was talking to one group of people.

'What has happened?' Sido asked, his voice ringing out in the stillness.

Mala explained to him about the visit of some tribesmen and about Kanhu leaving with them, including the fact that he had taken his sword. Sido's expression darkened as he absorbed the reality of the situation—his brother facing the might of Madho. He feared that Kanhu's reckless behaviour would only escalate the already volatile situation.

Without a moment's hesitation, Sido rallied with two young men on his journey to the other town. He instructed his younger brothers to stay behind and keep watch over the village. The urgency in his voice was palpable as he set off at a brisk pace, determined to catch up with Kanhu and put an end to the madness.

As Sido and the young men walked through the countryside, he couldn't shake the feeling of unease that had settled in the pit of his stomach. His mind raced with questions, trying to understand why Kanhu would act so impulsively.

Twenty years ago, Sido's world had turned upside down when his father had passed away and the notorious moneylender, Madho Soren, had arrived at their doorstep, demanding immediate repayment of a loan, along with the threat that he would seize their entire estate. Sido was a boy then, but the sight of his mother's desperate cries and his helplessness had sparked a determination within him to do whatever it took to repay the debt. Sido had made a deal with Madho and impressively repaid the loan in just

SIDO KANHU

five months. The notorious moneylender was initially annoyed but ultimately impressed by Sido's determination and honesty.

As Sido jogged through the village, his mind was consumed with thoughts about his past and the change in his brother's behaviour.

As soon as he arrived in the village, he was faced with the sight of his fellow Santhals bleeding and being beaten by Madho's men.

In front of Madho's house, angry villagers were shouting insults and throwing stones at the wealthy landlord, who appeared on his balcony surrounded by armed guards. Sido searched the crowd for Kanhu and was relieved to find him, but concerned for his safety as he was aggressively walking towards Madho's house. Sido's attention quickly shifted to two men who were dragging two children, one of them a little girl who was crying and struggling to break free.

'Kanhu! We have to do something! Those children need our help,' Sido exclaimed.

Kanhu nodded in agreement, 'I'll go speak with Madho. Maybe we can come to a peaceful resolution.'

Sido watched as Kanhu walked towards the balcony, but his heart sank when he saw Madho's angry expression.

'What do you want, Kanhu?' Madho demanded.

'We're here to negotiate for the release of the children,' Kanhu replied calmly.

Madho scowled, 'I don't negotiate with peasants. Leave now before I have my men attack.'

Suddenly, a guard nocked an arrow and aimed it towards Kanhu. The shot flew past him, causing panic among the villagers.

'Stop!' Kanhu shouted, 'We don't want any violence. We just want those children to be returned to their families.'

Madho bellowed, challenging Kanhu to fight like a true warrior. He threatened to shoot arrows and kill everyone if they dared touch his men.

'We won't back down!' Sido shouted, 'We'll fight for what's right and just!'

Kanhu stood firm, 'We are not leaving without those children. You may have money and power, but we have something you don't—the courage to stand up for our people!'

The tension in the air was palpable as the two sides seemed ready for a face-off, each unwilling to back down. It was a battle between ones who believed in justice and ones who were blinded by greed and power.

Kanhu didn't waste a single moment as he launched himself towards the guard who tried to reload his bow. His sword swung through the air, just missing the guard's fingers.

However, Kanhu had made a fatal error. Without him noticing, other guards had encircled him, trapping him in a circle of steel. Five men with swords stood ready to take him down. Kanhu swung his blade with all his might, but the guards were skilled fighters and avoided his attack, retaliating with their own swords. The metallic ring echoed through the air as the blades clashed.

One of the guards kicked Kanhu in the back, sending him sprawling to the ground with a painful groan. The guards paused, their swords pointed at him. Madho laughed triumphantly, enjoying the scene. Sido immediately got down on his knees in front of the moneylender and pleaded for his brother's life.

'I will spare him, but under one condition,' Madho said with a cruel smile. 'He needs to be taught a lesson.'

Sido's desperate voice asked, 'What condition?'

'Let my men do their bit, and he won't fight back.'

In spite of Sido's exhortation, Kanhu stubbornly tried to get back up. The guards overpowered him, holding him down and taking away his sword. One of them had a firm grip around his neck. Sido pleaded Kanhu to surrender, but he refused.

'I am your elder brother. Please think of your family,' Sido tried to instill a sense of understanding in him.

Kanhu's strength was beginning to wane. He looked into his brother's eyes and saw fear. With a sigh, he stopped fighting and allowed the guards to tie his hands. They started to beat him, but he took the beating without resistance, gritting his teeth and bearing the pain in silence.

Madho smiled in satisfaction and signalled for his orderly to come forward. Madho whispered something in his ear and the orderly disappeared back into the house.

Sido's heart raced with fear as he watched the orderly come out from the house carrying a blade. Within a few minutes, the crisp sound of the blade shaving Kanhu's hair filled the air. In less than ten minutes, Kanhu's once proud mane was reduced to a stubble. His face had cuts and was bleeding from the rough handling of the blade.

The villagers tried to move forward, but Sido held them back. He wanted to save his brother, but he didn't know how. He was frozen, unable to say the word 'no', and instead, he bowed in defeat.

Madho watched from a distance, a smug smile spreading

across his face. He believed that this act of humiliation would teach the villagers a lesson. As his men brought out the captive children, the parents wept in despair. The boy, around eight years old, and the five-year-old girl screamed in joy as they were left on the ground. The villagers handed over coins and grains of rice to Madho's men, hoping to save their children.

Soren came down from his roof, accompanied by more men. The village suddenly fell silent. Turning to the villagers, he warned, 'You have seen the power of money. It can even buy the lives of innocents. You can live peacefully with us or continue to oppose us. Choose wisely.'

The sound of the blade running over Kanhu's scalp finally stopped. Madho's men released Kanhu, and he stumbled towards Sido, who caught him in a warm embrace. Madho's threat had weakened the resolve of the villagers, and they scattered, leaving him and his men to revel in their victory. Madho instructed his men to release the children and warned the parents that they had one week to pay or would have to give their cattle away if they are not able to. The parents of the captive children took their sobbing offsprings in their arms, grateful for their safe return.

For now, there was peace in the village, but Sido knew it was only temporary. The oppressive landlord and his men would not rest until they had complete control over their lives.

Countdown to Revolution
00:00:01

45 days before the Hul
Late evening, May 1855
Bhognadih

The sky hung over them like a thick curtain of indigo, with only the flickering flames of the campfire to break the darkness. The forest around them was alive with the sounds of nocturnal creatures, but the group of Santhals remained quiet, lost in their own thoughts.

Sido sat with his back against a tree, his eyes fixed on the fire. Kanhu was beside him, sharpening his machete, the sound of metal rubbing against stone filling the air. A few feet away, a group of elders were huddled together, worry etched on their faces.

Meanwhile, Sido's wife, Mala, and his sisters, Phulo and Jano, were making preparations for dinner back home. The aroma filled the air, promising a meal that would soothe their rumbling stomachs.

The Murmu brothers had gathered a group of like-minded Santhals, and they were camped deep in the forest, far away from the prying eyes of the British and their collaborators. Sido and Kanhu knew that they could not continue living in subjugation. They had seen too many of their fellow Santhals fall prey to the moneylenders and their agents. The incident with Madho had been the final nail in the coffin. It had been terrifying facing the might and money power of the zamindar but they were out of all other options. It was time to take a stand, to fight for their freedom and their way of life.

As Sido looked around at the faces of his comrades, he could see the desperation in their eyes. They had all suffered at the hands of the moneylenders, forced to toil in the fields daily, their hard-earned wages snatched away from them by the greedy landlords and rapacious officials.

'We cannot continue like this,' Sido said, his voice calm and measured, breaking the silence. 'We must take action.'

The group turned to face Sido as he continued to speak. 'We have suffered long enough. We have seen our brothers and sisters beaten, our children go hungry. We cannot allow this to continue.'

The Santhals nodded in agreement, their faces reflecting their shared pain and desperation. But they were also wary, knowing the risks involved in challenging the British and their allies.

'What can we do?' one of the Santhals asked, his voice tinged with doubt.

Sido looked around at the group, with an unwavering gaze. 'We can fight. We can stand up to these oppressors and demand our freedom.'

The others looked at him with a mix of hope and uncertainty. They knew that the British and their lackeys would not take kindly to a group of Santhals challenging their authority. But they also knew that they had nothing left to lose.

'Sido is right,' Kanhu said firmly. 'We cannot sit back and let these moneylenders and their allies continue to exploit us. We must take action, and we must do it now.'

The other Santhals murmured their assent. Sido listened intently, his sharp eyes scanning the faces of his comrades. He knew that they were all feeling the same desperation that he was. They had all suffered long enough. It was time for them to take action.

After holding their discussion, when the group dispersed, someone touched Sido's shoulder. He turned to find Mala staring at him with concern. 'What are you planning, Sido?' she asked in a low voice.

He hesitated for a moment about whether he should tell her about their collective decision, but couldn't keep it from her. She was his partner in life and his equal in every way, and so he told her, 'We are planning to take action against the moneylenders.' As he said that, he looked for any traces of fear on her face.

Mala's expression remained the same. She simply said, 'I will help you in any way I can.' Sido loved his wife and now had another reason to be proud of her. She was as brave and as dedicated to their cause as any man in their tribe.

He knew he could count on her and his sisters, who had also participated in their discussion. They would each take on different roles in their plan, sharing the responsibilities among themselves. Sido's mind raced as he walked back to his hut. He knew their plan would be difficult, but it was necessary to carry it out successfully. The forest was their ally and they knew it well. They had lived in harmony with nature for generations, and they were skilled at navigating the dense foliage and avoiding detection.

The following day, as they gathered around the fire one more

SIDO KANHU

time, Sido started to outline their plan. The Santhals listened attentively, their faces reflecting a mix of fear and determination.

As he went to bed that night, Sido knew that the path ahead would be challenging, but he was determined to see it through for his people, his family and himself. The fire crackled, casting shadows on the faces of the Santhals, all of whom lay huddled around. Sido closed his eyes and took a deep breath. The fate of his people now depended on him.

33 days before the Hul
Early morning, May 1855
Bhognadih

The morning sun had just begun to shine through the thin bamboo sticks that made up the walls of the hut, casting its light on the bed made from bamboo leaves. Sido lay there, listening to the sound of raindrops pattering against the roof. The leaves of the trees and vines twitched in the gentle breeze outside his open window as if they had a life of their own.

But Sido's peace was suddenly disrupted as he saw a tall figure approach him. He gasped as he took in the sight of the man covered in ashes. This was no ordinary man, Sido realized, but Marang Buru, their deity.

Sido felt his legs buckle as he knelt in reverence and awe, whispering, 'Thakur...' He knew he had found his home and his deity.

'My son,' Thakur said softly. His voice was calming and wise, filling Sido with a sense of peace. The thunder outside the hut acted as a gentle accompaniment to Thakur's words.

'I have a message for you, my child. Come closer,' Thakur said. Sido walked closer, dazed.

'My child,' Thakur said, his eyes calm and wise. 'Your strength lies in your faith. Trust the gods, believe in yourself and never forget the power of love. You have a special place in this world and it is up to you to take it.'

Sido felt his chest swell with a newfound determination. He knew that this was his home and his fate—to protect and serve the people of his village, to keep them safe and to serve their faith. The gods had chosen him to be the protector of this village, and he would do everything in his power not to disappoint them.

As the thunder grew to a crescendo, Thakur pointed towards the heavens, and Sido felt a wave of peace rush over him. He heard the message loud and clear, and felt a deep sense of peace and purpose in his heart that had been absent before.

With a smile, he thanked the deity for his guidance and stepped out into the world, ready to create a better future for himself and his people.

Sido awoke with a start, his heart pounding in his chest. He looked around and realized that he was back in his bed, surrounded by the familiar walls of his hut. He rubbed his eyes and took a deep breath, trying to calm himself. Slowly, the events of his dream came back to him, leaving behind a sense of awe. The message from Marang Buru was still fresh in his mind and he knew that it was a divine sign. With a smile, he got out of his bed and thanked the gods for their guidance. He was filled with a newfound determination to follow his purpose and serve his village.

21 days before the Hul
Afternoon, June 1855
Bhognadih

The four Murmu brothers sat cross-legged on the ground, surrounded by hazy dust. Sido, the eldest, spoke with a quiet urgency that drew the attention of his siblings. Kanhu, Chand and Bhairab leaned in, their eyes fixed on their brother's face.

Sido's voice was soft but clear, and he spoke of his dream. He shared how his son, too, had felt the call to fight against the British and the moneylenders. His brothers listened with rapt attention, their expressions shifting from curiosity to awe.

'This is a divine message,' Sido declared, his voice ringing with conviction. 'A message from our Thakur to stand up for what is right.'

Chand spoke up, his words tumbling out with a sense of urgency. 'I've been hearing a voice in my mind for days now. I didn't understand it at first, but after hearing what Sido just told us, I know it was a message from Thakur.'

Bhairab's eyes widened with curiosity. He leaned forward and asked, 'What did the message say?'

'"Go out and find me",' Chand replied.

The brothers exchanged glances, realizing the significance

of the message. They spoke of the omens they had seen, and believed that Thakur was instructing them to fight against the British and the moneylenders. Sido acknowledged their questions, slowly spoke, with his words carrying a weight of truth, 'We cannot rely on the British courts or the moneylenders. They don't care about us or our villages. They only care about what they can take from us. We've tried the courts and appeals, and it's gotten us nowhere. We need to stand together and fight for what's right. We have Thakur with us and that's all we need.'

The brothers nodded in agreement, understanding the gravity of the situation. They decided to spread the message to all the members of their clan, calling for a gathering after the upcoming twenty nights. Sido suggested sending the message using an old method—carving out symbols on Sal branches—something only the Santhals could understand.

'Marang Buru will protect us while we fight for our land and our people. We'll show them the strength of our devotion,' Sido said in an unwavering voice.

The brothers stood up, their faces determined as they set out to spread the message by carrying across the branches and handing them over to their allies in secrecy. The wind blew, stirring the dust and leaves around them, and the distant sound of a beating drum echoed through the trees, signalling the start of a new chapter in their history.

The message was: 'Fellow brothers and sisters, gather in the field of Bhognadih on the full moon day of the month of Ashar. There is also a message from Thakur to be shared. I will share when we all meet.'

One day before the Hul
Early night, 30 June 1855
Jungles of the Santhal Land

The room was bathed in an eerie stillness, the only sound being the measured ticking of the grandfather clock—a ghostly reminder of the fleeting nature of time. The walls were adorned with portraits of long-dead men, their eyes following Commissioner Brown as he entered the room. The beds had not been slept in for months. A single lamp flickered on the wall, casting ominous shadows over empty picture frames that once held the images of young, beautiful women, now long gone.

One portrait caught Brown's attention. It was that of a woman with a wide smile who was wearing an oversized pair of glasses. Her pale complexion matched the tiny flowers on her blue dress, and a small, golden object could be seen clutched between her hands. As Brown turned towards the window, his reflection in the glass seemed to waver, an unsettling sight that left him feeling uneasy.

In the treacherous jungles, a bit far from the Santhal villages, Brown and Vincent had taken up residence in a makeshift house. Brown ordered tea and began to write letters, pausing to converse with Vincent before turning to the pile of papers kept on the table in front of him. The night was illuminated by the moon, but it was not enough to make out the contents of the documents.

As they were sorting through the papers, news arrived that many Santhals were gathering at a nearby location—they had an informer among the Santhals. Brown knew that he needed to act quickly and ordered Vincent to leave the room because he did not want him to know about the details of the situation owing to his relationship with Mina. Once he was left alone, a ragged young Santhal man from Mina's village was brought in by one of his men. The man looked terrified, his eyes darting around the room as he clutched his tattered clothes.

'Tell me what you know,' Brown said in a low commanding voice. The man hesitated, clearly afraid for his life. Brown leaned forward, his eyes narrowing, and repeated his question. Finally, the man spoke, revealing some details.

Meanwhile, Vincent waited outside the room, his senses on high alert. The only sound he could hear was the soft rustling of leaves as the wind whispered through the trees. Suddenly, he heard the door open and the sound of footsteps approaching. The guards saluted as Brown emerged, his face set in determination. Vincent couldn't help but feel a sense of foreboding as he watched Brown walk out into the moonlit fields, his silhouette a stark reminder of the danger that lay ahead.

The day of the Great Rally before the Hul
Night, 30 June 1855
Field near Bhognadih

The massive gathering of Santhals bathed in the silver glow of the full moon. The message conveyed by the Murmu brothers had spread rapidly, stirring the hearts of many clans and inspiring them to chant in unison, 'Let's go to Bhognadih!' Young and old, men and women, including those with disabilities, had all come together for this historic gathering.

Sido and Kanhu stood among the sea of people, their eyes scanning the crowd. Kanhu leaned in towards Sido's ear, his voice barely above a whisper, 'How many do you think have assembled here, brother?'

'As far as the eye can see,' Sido replied with a sense of awe.

'More are coming,' Phulo added.

'Yes, more are coming. We'll wait a little longer, let more people gather around us,' Sido said. With the help of members from different villages and regions, they estimated that there were close to ten thousand people in attendance.

Sido stepped forward, the bow and arrow across his bare chest a testament to his bravery. Raising his arms, he began to speak, 'My dear brothers and sisters, you are all my kin. Our families have lived together for centuries, we've tilled the land, honoured our traditions, and our Thakur has always blessed us in our endeavours.'

The crowd nodded in agreement, their eyes fixed on Sido as he continued, 'But evil has come in the form of the mahajans, the moneylenders. They have taken our land, taxed us heavily, and subjected our families and loved ones to unspeakable atrocities.' Sido's voice rose, 'Sometimes, I wonder why we must endure this pain. But then it became clear—it is all a test from our Thakur, Lord Marang Buru. Now you may ask how do I know this? It is because I met him.'

A hushed silence fell over the crowd, their murmurs of excitement and disbelief growing louder as they whispered to each other, 'He met Thakur!', 'Is it possible?', 'Is Thakur here?'.

Sido raised his hand, silencing the crowd. 'Yes, our Thakur, Lord Marang Buru, came to me in a dream. We had a conversation, and he reminded me that he loves us,' he declared.

The murmurs started again, gradually dying down as Sido continued, 'He loves us and is testing us to see if we will change in the face of evil or hold true to our beliefs. Our beliefs define us, and we were never meant to live as we do now, paying such high taxes and *lagan* on our hard-earned labour.'

A voice called out, 'Yes, it's true!'

Sido turned towards the voice, 'Yes, it's true. Thakur told me that we should decide how much to pay, and if we feel like it, we shouldn't pay anything at all. But in this new world, if we must give something, and when we do, we should expect something in return.'

Several voices around the area echoed, 'Yes, we should expect something in return.'

Sido spread his arms wide, 'We will decide what we need to pay. And we will decide whether we need to pay. We will take back our freedom from the moneylenders.'

The Santhals knew that while the British had created the law, the local police were using it to arrest those who were unfamiliar with it because they enjoyed using the law to intimidate and threaten the Santhals, citing contracts from moneylenders to claim that the Santhals owed them debts, which meant they couldn't complain. The police were using these contracts and rules to threaten the Santhals with jail time or higher fines, and the Santhals were left with no option but to meekly comply. Now, it was decided that they would not give in.

Sido stood on the elevated stony surface, taking in the sea of faces before him. His eyes searched the crowd, searching for the voice that had risen above the rest. He found the source. It was a middle-aged man, standing in the front row shouting at the top of his lungs, 'Let us remember the poem, the poem that was born from our pain.' Sido motioned for the man to come forward, to recite the poem that spoke of their struggles.

The man stepped forward, reciting the words of the poem with fierce conviction:

> 'Saheb rule is full of trouble.
> Shall we go or shall we stay?
> Eating, drinking and clothing—
> For everything, we face trouble.
> Shall we go or shall we stay?

SIDO KANHU

> Sido, why are you bathed in blood?
> Kanhu, why do you cry, 'Hul', 'Hul'?
> For our people, we have bathed in blood,
> for the trader thieves.'

Sido listened intently, nodding his head in agreement. The words of the poem struck a chord within him, reminding him of the injustices they had suffered for far too long. He turned to the crowd and said, 'It is time for us to run things on our own. The time has come for us to take an oath to protect our jungles, our lands, our motherland.' The crowd erupted in a thunderous cheer, their voices united in a common cause.

Sido knew that the journey ahead would not be easy. But with the support of the crowd behind him, he felt a glimmer of hope. Some were hesitant to leave their families behind, but Sido reassured them that they were not expected to abandon their homes completely but keep moving across the frontlines and come back home, based on how the revolution progresses. They were all striving to move forward to create a better future for their children.

Just then, a man approached Sido, introducing himself as Kishore Singh, the leader of another clan. 'My people are ready to support the cause, to stand by you in any way they can,' Singh said with a bow.

Sido turned to him with a warm smile, 'Thank you for coming, brother. We need warriors like you.'

The chant of 'Thakur, Thakur, Thakur' grew louder and more insistent. Sido raised his voice, addressing the crowd once more, 'Now, let's get ready to meet our Thakur in person. Let's go to the hills and make our homes strong. Let's build a fortress around ourselves, so no one can harm us while we wage a war.' The crowd rose as one, ready to follow Sido on this journey towards freedom.

The assembly of Santhals eagerly waited for Sido to continue. He raised his voice to address them. 'We must open our hearts and extend a warm welcome to our Thakur, who conveyed his message to us,' he said, eliciting a rousing cheer from the crowd. 'And when He arrives, we will celebrate our homecoming with a song, one we have not sung since we left the forests.'

Sido could see the worry etched on the faces of some of the people, so he sought to ease their fears. 'I know many of you are concerned about your future, but have faith. Our Thakur, Lord Marang Buru, is working behind the scenes to ensure that no one is exploited and all are treated as equals. The jungle will be our salvation.'

With the crowd's spirits boosted, Sido and Kanhu divided them into groups and appointed leaders, with titles such as 'subhas' and 'darogas'. The assembly took an oath, under the leadership of Sido and Kanhu, to fight against any form of oppression. The Thakur's name echoed through the air, fueling their excitement.

In a hushed tone, Sido revealed a secret to the crowd, 'My friends, I have something important to share with you. We must move quickly and remain hidden in the forests. Make plans and prepare yourselves, for each one of us is a leader. In times of hardship, it is easy to lose our strength, but we must not forget our power.'

He continued, 'I urge you to spread the word to your friends and families, so they, too, can make an informed decision to join the revolution. Real change can occur only when the truth is known. Come together as one family, one community and one nation, in the name of our freedom.'

The crowd's cheers of 'Hul! Hul! Hul!' grew louder as Sido delivered his call to action. He ordered half of them to march to the power centres of the moneylenders and the British, and overthrow them. And soon, news of the uprising spread like wildfire, igniting the spark of hope in every Santhal.

1 July 1855
Post-midnight
Bhognadih

'Hul! Hul!'

The chants of the ten thousand people gathered at Bhognadih sounded like music that invoked passion in the soul. The Santhals started stomping the ground with one foot gently, and the thumping sound hit and resonated across the place.

'Hul! Hul!'

'Hul! Hul!'

'*Karo ya maro* (Do or die).'

'*Angrezo hamri mati chodo* (Englishmen leave our soil).'

'Hul! Hul!'

'Hul! Hul!'

'*Karo ya maro.*'

'Hul! Hul!'

'Hul! Hul!'

The Santhals were a proud people, but they had grown tired of the injustice inflicted upon them by the oppressors and foreigners who treated them as mere property. Their anger fuelled their synchronized movements as they began stomping the ground with a unified beat, the sound resonating across the gathering.

Sido, dressed in white cloth and adorned with a green leaf, stood tall and raised his arms wide in a V-shape. With a voice ringing with authority, he shouted, 'Listen, brothers and sisters. Thakur has answered our prayers and brought us here today to reclaim what is rightfully ours. It's time to rise against these oppressors and show them our strength.'

Kanhu, with his emaciated features, stepped forward. In spite of his appearance, his hunger for change gave him wondrous strength. 'Thakur has appeared to us multiple times,' he declared with emotion. 'He saw our struggles and heard our cries. He wants us to stand together and say enough is enough. The dikus and white men treat us as though they are entitled, but where were they when our ancestors tilled this land? Everything they have is because of us, and this is how they repay us?'

As the night cooled and a gentle wind blew across their faces, the Santhals felt a sense of change in the air. Sido stood up and addressed the crowd, announcing their path to immortality. 'Today, I am announcing our path to unity. We work, toil and share everything together, and now we will bleed together for our families and future generations.'

The crowd erupted in applause, and Sido continued his speech. 'You are all witnesses to the tireless work of your brothers and sisters who have struggled under difficult conditions to ensure that we can live with dignity. But this injustice must come to an end.'

Sido then stepped down from the stage and knelt on his knees, placing his hands on the ground and closing his eyes. Watching this, everyone followed suit, becoming still and silent in reverence.

They were expressing their gratitude to the earth, which had once been filled with tall bushes and dangerous creatures but was now the home of the Santhals.

For too long, the Santhals had been agreeable. They had accepted unjust taxes for over thirty years, which had forced them to take loans from greedy moneylenders. Sido declared he wouldn't stand any of it any longer. 'We will only give them what we want to give,' he declared. 'But if they refuse this agreement, we will fight them to death.'

Sido raised his bow and arrow, and the crowd readied themselves to march, chanting 'Let's go to Kalikata!' They were determined to show the moneylenders and other exploiters seated at the helm of the East India Company what they were made of and demand an answer right away. The wind of change was blowing, and the Santhals were ready to make their stand.

2 July 1855
Sometime in the afternoon
Bhognadih

Sido and Kanhu stood frozen, staring at each other with expressions of shock and anger as they heard the news of Bijoy Manjhi's death in Bhagalpur jail. Bijoy was one of their own, a fellow Santhal, and now he was gone. But the shock only deepened as they learnt that two more of their people had been arrested by the local police for protesting against Bijoy's death. The news came from another group of Santhals who were joining the movement.

'It's Mahesh Dutta again, that corrupt police officer,' Kanhu raged, and Sido could see the hatred in his eyes. Mahesh Lal Dutta was well known to the Santhals. He was a police officer in charge of the Dighi area. He was notorious for collaborating with moneylenders to collect revenue by force. If the Santhals didn't pay up, they faced torture or arrest.

Sido and Kanhu were filled with outrage at the thought of their people being mistreated by the local police. 'They never needed a reason to mistreat us before,' Sido replied calmly, his voice barely hiding the anger boiling inside him. 'And now we have no reason to hold back.'

The situation only worsened as they learnt that two more of their compatriots had been arrested on charges of fraud, which was brought forward by Madho.

In the sleepy village of Litipara, the sound of discontent had started to rise. Bijoy, a resident of the village, had taken a loan of twelve baskets of rice from Madho, who also acted as a local trader. Even after he received ten baskets from Bijoy, the debt was far from paid in Madho's eyes. He had demanded more and when Bijoy had refused to meet with him, he had arrived at Bijoy's house with his musclemen to seize the house and land. Many villagers had gathered, making noise, but could not attack Madho. However, they did manage to ensure that Bijoy was left unharmed by Madho and his men.

But Madho was not done. A few days later, he had returned with even more force. This time, he had more musclemen along with the local police, led by Mahesh Daroga. The villagers were powerless to defend themselves as they had limited weapons. Madho and Mahesh had arrested Bijoy and taken him to Bhagalpur jail, where he had been subjected to torture until he died. No justice was served and instead more villagers were arrested or beaten for protesting against the cruelty meted out to Bijoy. Madho had, by then, seized the lands of two more villagers, sparking outrage among the people.

When the news of these events reached Sido and Kanhu, they were incensed. It was no longer just about the land and properties, but about self-respect.

'No more,' Sido hissed under his breath, spitting on the ground in disgust. 'Curse befall the dikus!' he swore, his anger boiling at the thought of the moneylenders having free rein to do as they pleased with their wealth.

'We've got to go get them,' Kanhu said, his eyes blazing with determination. They were determined to learn more about the death of Bijoy and the recent arrests, uncover the truth and fight for justice for their people.

'Change of plans!' he declared loudly. The Santhals turned to look at him in surprise. 'That evil and corrupt man, Madho Soren, has taken the help of Mahesh Daroga and arrested our friends, Garbu and Harma Manjhi. And although that greedy bastard had already seized Garbu's properties, he's taken Harma's too! We only have our respect left now. What else do they want? We will not let them take anything else from us now!'

The people erupted in a chant of 'Hul, Hul, Hul!' in unison, thrusting their bows and arrows up towards the sky. The fire of discontent had been sparked, and the Santhals were determined to make a stand. They would march to Bhagalpur, where the Manjhis were being taken and not leave until Mahesh set them free. Out of all the hundreds of people marching alongside the Murmus, not one hesitated. The Manjhis represented all of them and they were willing to do whatever it took to fight for their self-respect and dignity. Instead of heading to Kalikata, they would now go to Bhagalpur, and this journey was only the beginning of their fight for justice.

3 July 1855
Afternoon
Burhait Bazaar, Bhagalpur

The sun shone mercilessly while the Santhals waited patiently by the dusty road leading to Burhait Bazaar in Bhagalpur. They had been there for a few hours, their stomachs empty and their throats dry. But they were determined to see justice served.

As they waited, they strategized, dividing themselves into groups and taking up positions at different points. They knew that this was the only way to stop Madho Soren and the corrupt police chief, Mahesh, from passing through with their captives.

When Madho finally arrived, the Santhals sprang into action, forming a human barricade around him and his prisoners. They outnumbered Madho's men, being armed with bows, arrows, axes and spears. But Madho was drunk on power and thought he was invincible with Mahesh and his men by his side.

'What's all this about!' Madho shouted, his voice shaking with rage.

'We demand that you release the Manjhis and return their properties to them. They have done nothing wrong,' Sido shouted back.

Madho's ugly grin spread across his face, his decaying teeth visible. 'You're all fools,' he sneered. 'Next, you'll ask us to get down on our knees and beg for our lives, and that is when you'll all die.'

But the Santhals were not intimidated. They stood their ground, their eyes fixed on Madho and Mahesh. The arrested Manjhis, bleeding from their heads, looked on in shock, but also with a glimmer of hope in their eyes.

Phulo, Sido's elder sister, stepped forward from the crowd. 'We are not alone,' she said. 'The moon goddess is with us. And justice will prevail.'

With these words, the Santhals surged forward, their weapons raised, ready to fight for what was right. The tension in the air was palpable as the fate of the Manjhis and the corrupt officials hung in the balance.

Phulo's face flushed with anger and she tightened her grip on her weapon, a short blade, as the crowd swelled around her. 'All I want is justice,' she said through gritted teeth.

Madho shouted, 'Listen to me, you peasants! If you don't let us pass, I'll have you all arrested!'

Sido's eyes narrowed, and his blood boiled. 'How dare you threaten us!' he shouted. 'Look around you! We're the ones making the demands here. And we demand that you release the Manjhis and listen to us! Or we'll rescue them by force!'

Several hundred Santhals stepped forward from the crowd, ready to face Madho and his men. The air was thick with tension and the sound of unsheathed knives.

As the police chief's men reached for their weapons, Garbu

sprang forward and grabbed an axe from one of the Santhals. He shouted, 'Hul! Hul!' and lunged towards Madho. The latter took out a sword and swung it across wildly. But his blows fell short. As he backed away, he stumbled and fell. Garbu jumped on this opportunity and hit Madho in the head using the axe. Madho's skull cracked open, and he fell from his carriage, his eyes wide and unseeing. A hail of arrows followed, flying towards Madho's men before they could even raise their weapons.

As Madho's lifeless body lay on the dusty road, the Santhals erupted into cheers and cries of victory. Garbu stood over him, his chest heaving with adrenaline, his axe dripping with blood. The Manjhis were free at last and justice had been served.

Phulo led the Santhals in a dance of celebration, her eyes shining with pride and relief. The sun had started its descent towards the horizon, casting a warm glow on those gathered. The captives, bruised and battered, hugged their rescuers, tears streaming down their faces.

Sido felt a surge of relief as he watched his people cheer in celebration. He joined them.

As they marched towards Panchkatia, the group of rebels grew in number, bolstered by those who shared their cause. They were a determined lot, with their eyes fixed on the prize: to reclaim the land and property that was rightfully theirs, which had been snatched away by the greedy moneylenders and merchants who had exploited them for far too long.

The rebels moved with purpose, their resolve unshakeable. They had trained and fought together for months and were battle-hardened. Though they knew the risks involved in their mission, they were willing to face them head-on.

As they approached the outskirts of the town, the rebels split into smaller groups and launched simultaneous attacks on the businesses of the moneylenders and merchants, showing no mercy to their foes. They fought with all their might, using their bows and arrows, swords and other weapons to take down their enemies.

The sound of battle echoed through the streets as the rebels clashed with their rivals. They fought fiercely, with each blow struck in the name of justice and reclaiming their birthright. The merchants and moneylenders fought back, but they were no match for the determination and strength of the rebels.

In spite of their best efforts, the merchants and moneylenders were pushed back, with many among them killed as the Santhals advanced. The Santhals continued their march towards the heart of Panchkatia.

As the dust settled, the Santhals emerged victorious. They had shown their oppressors that they would no longer be pushed around. And they marched on, their heads held high, ready to take on any challenge that came their way.

5 July 1855
Morning
Few kilometres away from Bhagalpur

The air in the room was tense as Commissioner Brown's steely gaze swept over the officers, each one feeling the weight of their duty to protect the colony. The wooden floorboards creaked as they shifted in their seats, uneasy with the news of the Santhals' violent uprising.

Brown stood tall, his starched uniform immaculate and his posture erect. His eyes were fixed on one of Madho Soren's men, who trembled under his intense scrutiny.

'Tell us everything you know,' Brown ordered in a low, controlled voice.

The man, who had come to relay the information to the officers and the commissioner, recounted the horrors he had witnessed. 'It was chaos, Commissioner. The Santhals were like animals, hacking and slashing with their axes. The police chief was the first to go and then the rest of our men were killed. They took over our villages and are claiming them as their own. And now they're coming for us, Commissioner. They want our blood.'

The room erupted in murmurs of fear and uncertainty.

Brown's jaw tightened, his mind racing as he contemplated their next move.

'Where are they now?' he demanded to know.

The man hesitated, fear etched on his face. 'They're on the move, Commissioner. Heading for Bhagalpur. We must evacuate immediately.'

Brown's mind was made up. 'We will not back down or give in to these savages,' he declared, his voice booming with conviction. 'We will defend our colony and protect our people. Send out a call for gathering arms. We will not be defeated by a group of tribals.'

Brown stopped pacing across the partially carpeted floor and barked orders at the man in front of him, who quickly nodded and turned to leave. Before he could make it out the door, Brown called him back, 'Wait! Who is leading them?'

'The Murmu family, all the siblings. But Sido and Kanhu are the heads of the rebellion,' he confirmed before hurrying away.

Brown muttered to himself, 'Those wretched idiots,' as he thought of the Santhals as nothing more than workhorses.

Three hours later, Major Tom Baroj appeared in full uniform with a red hat and white pants, standing at attention before Brown. 'Commissioner,' he addressed him.

Brown crooked his finger, calling Baroj forward, and said in a lowered voice, 'Listen to me.' As he spoke, his mint breath wafted on to Baroj's face. 'The Santhals have forgotten who their leaders are and are headed here on a mad mission. I want men positioned all over Bhagalpur and Rajmahal Hills. Make sure they do not cross over. Do whatever it takes. Do you hear me?'

'Yes, Sir,' Baroj replied. 'They will not enter. I reached slightly late here because I was busy dispatching two battalions ahead—around a hundred armed men and some twenty horsemen.'

'Good,' Brown said, pleased. 'I will back your decision.' They shook hands, and then Brown's eyes darkened as he added, 'One more thing.'

Baroj straightened up, 'Yes, Sir?'

'If you get hold of Sido or Kanhu, bring them to me. I want their heads!' Brown's voice shook with intensity.

Baroj accepted the command and saluted him before turning to walk out. As he reached the door, he turned back to face Brown and said, 'Don't worry, Sir. I have a backup plan if I don't get them alive.'

Watching Baroj depart, Brown thought, *No wonder I like this guy. He takes proactive decisions.*

7 July 1855
Evening
Kahalgaon

The dust from Baroj's horse swirled around him as he rode into Kahalgaon, his heart pounding in his chest. He had been tasked with bringing the Santhal tribe to heel, but the sight that greeted him was not something he had expected. The Santhals were not just angry, they were fighting back with a vengeance. They were armed, and their army numbered in the thousands. Even though they had rifles, Baroj and his troops were outnumbered, and he realized that they stood no chance against the enemy.

With a heavy heart, Baroj made the decision to retreat and regroup. He led his troops to safety, away from the prying eyes of the Santhal army, where he could send a letter to Brown, updating him on the situation.

Baroj wrote in a frantic scrawl, 'Commissioner, we need more men. A lot more. The Santhal army is armed and guarding every area. They are angry and out of their minds, Commissioner. Unless we can outnumber them, we stand no chance. The situation is worse than we thought. Please send troops, so that we can carry out your orders. I will hold my position on the heights and wait for the Nawab's army to arrive. Long Live the Queen. Thanking you, Major Baroj.'

The letter reached Brown, and he hissed under his breath as he read it. Baroj was now seen as incompetent, and Brown realized that the situation was graver than what they had previously thought. The Santhals were not just retaliating, they were fighting back as a civilization.

With a sense of urgency, Brown quickly wrote a letter, addressed to the cantonment in Danapur. He informed them of the impending doom and requested more troops. The letter was received and Major General Daniel Lloyd was appointed to bring the rebellion under control, and the first step was to promote Colonel Bard, one of the most reliable servants of the Company, to the rank of a brigadier.

Brigadier Bard saluted his commanding officer with a sense of pride, thrilled to be given such a prestigious role. He was given charge of the districts of Bankura and Birbhum, and was told that he would also have an officer from the region to support local intelligence. The officer in question was Major Vincent Jervis, someone that Bard knew well, having served with him in the Afghanistan campaign two years prior.

Bard was informed that he would have a wide arsenal at his disposal, including troops and cavalry. But Brown had one more surprise in store. 'You will have many cannons,' he said, 'and, most importantly, war-trained elephants.'

Bard gave a gentle chuckle, his confidence swelling. 'Elephants,' he thought. 'We are going to stamp out this rebellion.'

9 July 1855
Late morning
Pakur Rajbari

Sido and Kanhu, with their band of brothers, sisters and fellow Santhals, marched towards Pakur Rajbari, near Bhagalpur. They were determined to rid the land of the oppressive rule of the pro-British zamindar who managed the estate, just as many others.

'Are we finally going to go inside the market?' Kanhu asked Sido, his eyes filled with a fiery determination.

'Yes,' Sido replied, his voice a low growl. 'We'll go there and get rid of the zamindars once and for all.'

The group of Santhals raised a battle cry and marched towards the zamindar's estate, ready to take back what was rightfully theirs. But as they arrived, they encountered a shocking surprise—the zamindar and his possessions were nowhere to be found.

Sido cursed loudly, frustrated by the realization that their enemy had already fled. The Santhals, not ones to be discouraged, decided to send a message. They trashed the empty buildings, burning down whatever they could find, stealing valuable items and marking their territory with their tribal name. They then left Pakur Rajbari and headed towards Maheshpur, another land named after a zamindar.

'All of the zamindars will feel the pain they've inflicted on us for all these years,' Sido declared with confidence.

But little did they know about the danger that was nearing them. Bard, along with a large troop of British cavalry, war elephants and cannons, was headed straight for them. The Nawab of Murshidabad had also added his own contribution—five hundred cavalry soldiers, forty war elephants and cannons to the mix. The Santhals were marching into a storm and they were completely unaware of what awaited them.

10 July 1855
Early afternoon
Maheshpur

The dense jungle reverberated with the Santhals' determined march towards their next target, which was Maheshpur. Years of oppression and a burning desire for justice fuelled them, and the victories they had achieved so far inspired the youth of Pakur Rajbari, who were also Santhals, to join them.

As they approached the river, Sido felt a knot form in his stomach when he caught sight of a hundred British soldiers, armed with weapons far superior to anything they had ever seen. He had grown overconfident with their recent successes, but now, as he faced the reality of their enemy's might, fear washed over him.

Chand growled with anger, 'We should've seen this coming.'

'I know,' Sido replied, his voice heavy with frustration. 'I let my guard down and now we're facing the consequences.'

Bhairab, the second youngest brother, bellowed, 'Enough of this! We're not defeated yet. Let's fight!'

Jano, the only sister among them at the moment, stepped forward. In a clear tone, she said, 'My brothers, we've trained for this. We may die, but we'll die standing. Let's charge!'

Sido felt a surge of adrenaline as he led the charge towards the

British soldiers, shouting their battle cry, which echoed through the forest. His heart pounded in his chest as he raised his axe high, ready to strike. Around him, his fellow Santhals also charged, their arrows whistling through the air towards the enemy.

The clash was fierce, with the sound of gunfire and the clash of steel ringing through the trees. Sido dodged a bullet by a hair's breadth and charged towards the nearest soldier, swinging his axe with all his might. The soldier stumbled backwards, but many more were closing in on Sido. His senses were on high alert as he fought for his life, his eyes scanning the battlefield for any sign of his brothers and sister. He saw them fighting fiercely, their arrows flying true and their axes striking deep. But the cost of the battle was high, and the Santhals were losing ground.

In spite of the odds, Sido refused to give up. He knew that the Santhals' cause was just and that they had to fight to the bitter end. His heart swelled with pride as he saw his fellow warriors fight with all their might, their determination and bravery shining through the chaos of the battle.

As the battle raged on, Sido's mind was focussed on one thing: victory. He knew that the Santhals had to win this battle, that it was their only hope for freedom. His muscles ached and his lungs hurt, but he refused to give up. He fought with everything he had, determined to make a difference in the fate of his people. But in the end, despite their valiant efforts, the Santhals were forced to retreat. Sido and his brothers escaped with only a few injuries, but the loss of their fellow warriors weighed heavily on their hearts. Sido knew that the battle was not over, that they would have to fight again and again, until they won their freedom.

SIDO KANHU

In Dumka, Tribhuban and Mansingh Manjhi were leading another group of Santhals, and they were not on the radar of the British soldiers yet. As they approached the Nilkuthi and the caretakers of the Indigo Fort, years of oppression boiled over and they struck back with a battle cry, reclaiming what was rightfully theirs. The Santhals sent a message to their oppressors that they would not be broken and justice would be theirs at last.

11 July 1855
Early morning
Jungles of the Santhal Land

The Santhals were shaken. The previous day had seen the loss of many of their own, and Sido and his brothers were now leading the survivors back to their camp, their bodies battered and bloodied from the battle. The wounds, some from bullets and others from close combat, were a testament to the fight they had put up against the British soldiers and their allies.

However, the Santhals were far from defeated. Sido knew they needed to focus on avoiding the loss of lives of their tribesmen. He and his brothers had sent runners ahead to inform their supporters in different villages to prepare for war. Over the past two weeks, messages had been sent and plans had been put into place. The villages worked together to build a united front. As he scanned the area, he realized that they were deep in the jungle and needed rest.

After a good night's rest, as the sun rose, the Santhals sprang into action. Those with farming experience worked in the fields, hunters hunted for food and others made weapons and gathered supplies. Even though they were hiding in the jungles, they still returned to their villages for sustenance and recovery, and then came back to the camps. Everyone was contributing to the war in some way or the other. The Santhals had even established a backup plan, knowing that they would face resistance.

The camps were set up, and for a moment, everything seemed calm. But morning sun had brought with it a rude awakening. The sky was suddenly filled with anxiously chirping birds that were flying hither and thither in fear.

'They are here,' cried out Kanhu, as the Santhals readied themselves for battle.

The enemy approached, led by Major Baroj and his officers, intent on capturing the Santhals. But the Santhals were ready. Waiting like predators, they watched as the soldiers approached, clunky weapons giving away their attempt at a silent attack. As the soldiers got closer, the Santhals sprang forward, striking out with axes, arrows and swords. The soldiers cried out in pain as they were struck in their necks and heads, bleeding on the ground. Sido got hit in his thigh but continued to fight and lead the attack against Baroj.

A Santhal leader was struck down in the heat of the battle. He bellowed the word 'Hul' to his last breath, a rallying cry for liberty and a call for his people to keep fighting, even if he could not. The Santhals mourned as they watched their leader fall, their hearts boiling with anger and a thirst for vengeance.

The battle raged on as the Santhals roared and swung their weapons in a blind rage, but the British forces believed they had already won. However, they soon discovered their victory was short-lived as the surviving Santhals continued to fight, even when they were injured and dying, determined to take as many British soldiers down with them as possible. The British tried to stop the relentless charge, but more Santhals kept pouring in.

The sky suddenly darkened as ominous clouds gathered overhead, and the sound of thunder rumbled in the distance. The Santhal warriors and the British soldiers looked upward as a strong wind began to blow.

As the rain started to pour from the sky, the battle intensified. The ground was slick with mud and blood as both sides fought with unbridled ferocity. The heavy rain made it difficult for guns to fire, and the British started to lose more men, including a Major who was injured and pulled away from the frontlines. The Santhals pushed forward, taking advantage of the failure of the guns, and the tide began to turn in their favour. With their gunpowder wet, the British guns were all out of action and they had to rely on their swords. The Santhals were more vicious in close combat, and they began pushing back the British troops.

Suddenly, sound of a bugle echoed across the battlefield—the British had sounded the call to retreat. The red coats slowly backed away as the cannons fired and sometimes misfired from behind to cover their retreat.

The Santhals didn't celebrate their victory with song and dance. Instead, they were consumed by grief and exhaustion, sinking to the ground as their bodies shook. They stood in silence, the only sound being that of the moans of the wounded and the cries of mourners. They had won this round of the battle, but it had come at a great cost. The bodies of their fallen comrades lay scattered across the battlefield, some with arrows still protruding from their chests, while others had been trampled by horses or shot by bullets. The smell of blood and gunpowder hung heavy in the air, and the ground was slick with mud and gore.

The women of the village, who had not fought, came to the battlefield after the British retreated. They wailed and mourned for their husbands, sons and brothers, some collapsing in grief beside the lifeless bodies of their loved ones. The men who had survived moved from body to body, searching for any sign of life. But it was clear that many had died on the field that day.

Sido, who had been wounded but survived, looked upon the carnage with a heavy heart. He wondered if the cost of their rebellion had been too high, if their dreams of freedom were worth the lives of so many. Deep down, he knew that they had no choice but to fight for their rights, to resist the tyranny of the British Empire. As he knelt beside a body of a friend, he vowed to continue their struggle, to honour the sacrifice of those who had fallen and to never forget the price they were being forced to pay for their freedom.

12 July 1855
Early afternoon
Jungles of the Santhal Land

A day had passed since their recent confrontation with the British. Sido stood amidst the fallen bodies of his people, his heart heavy with their loss. He could still hear their cries echoing in his mind; their faces flashed in front of his eyes—they were the people he had grown up with; they laid their lives for the cause. All of this left him crestfallen. He suddenly broke the silence, 'Oh Thakur, what is your message for us?'

He closed his eyes and took a deep breath, the wind blowing in his face, helping to calm him. He opened his watery eyes and spoke firmly to the leaders gathered around him, 'We are not going to give up. Thakur wouldn't want us to.'

They sat in a circle surrounded by the bodies of their fallen comrades, a horrifying and unsettling sight. But Sido knew that they had to keep fighting to honour the spirits of their fallen comrades. He gestured to the bodies and asked, 'See all around you. Who are they? They are not dead bodies, they are spirited souls who gave their lives for our cause, a cause we must continue fighting for. They wouldn't have wanted us to give up.'

SIDO KANHU

Sido asked the leaders to prepare for the cremation and to be ready for any further attacks from the British. 'The British Army may have left for now, but the Company won't let it rest. They lost the fight and won't just sit quietly. They may start attacking villages and burning homes to show the rest of the country that we aren't safe anymore. We must take precautions and stay alert,' he warned.

Kanhu asked, 'Do we have a chance, brother?' Sido looked at him with fiery eyes and went to him, placing his hand on his shoulder. He needed to motivate not only Kanhu but all the Santhals.

'The British are the strongest in the world, and they will always find a way to survive. They are not just the enemy of the Santhals but of the entire world. They are the enemy of all that is good and true.' The Santhal warriors nodded in agreement. Sido continued, 'The Santhals are the protectors of this land and its people, the protectors of the earth and the protectors of the universe. Our mission is not to harm anyone, but to prevent harm from being inflicted on others. We are not here to burn or destroy, but to prevent destruction.'

The energy all around shifted visibly as the crowd cheered and chants of 'Hul, Hul' started echoing among the warriors. Sido raised his hand and continued, 'Our secret is out. The British know what we're capable of now, and they know we won't stop until the job is done. That's why they won't engage us head-on. I know we've lost many of our own, but if we stop now, we'll be abandoning not only our hopes but also that of the people we have been fighting for. The British may even be so afraid that they'll attack us with an army. But as long as we stand strong, we can fight back… I know that many of you want to return home to your families, but that isn't possible yet. The British are still here, waiting for an opportunity to strike back. We need to be smart, prepared, cautious, careful, quick, sharp, and most of all, brave.'

The air was filled with tension as Sido and the warriors stood at the forefront of the battle. Amidst the chaos and confusion, a voice rose from the crowd, 'We are strong! We are united!'

Sido stepped forward, his gaze sweeping across the sea of faces in front of him. He raised his hands, silencing the crowd and spoke with a voice that boomed across the battlefield. 'You are right, my fellow warrior. We are united, but the British are relentless and cunning. If we're not careful, if we're not smart, if we're not swift, if we're not brave, if we're not strong, they will defeat us. There is only one option, one way to protect our land and our people. We must win, no matter what comes our way.'

The warriors erupted into a frenzied chant, their voices echoing across the battlefield.

'We have to win no matter the loss.
'We have to win no matter the pain.
'We have to win no matter the tears.
'We have to win no matter the suffering.
'We have to win no matter the sacrifice.'

The warriors were infused with a spirit of determination and courage—their resolve to honour their fallen comrades and protect their land was unbreakable.

The next day, the sun beat down mercilessly, baking the

battlefield and bringing with it the unmistakable stench of death. The fallen Santhals were laid to rest and their bodies were bathed in the nearby river to wash away the blood and grime. The Santhals watched as the water purified their fallen brothers, leaving their bodies fresh and clean.

As the sun began to set, the Santhals lit a fire and burnt their dead. The smoke rose into the sky, creating a pillar of fire that blazed brighter and brighter with every passing minute. The crackling of the flames could still be heard in the air as the smoke ascended towards the heavens.

The Santhals watched the smoke rise in silence, their eyes misting with tears but their resolve unbroken. Sido felt the pain of his bullet wound once again, but he stood tall and led the warriors towards Katna village. The next day, they encountered resistance, but their enemy either eventually fled or was killed. For now, they had secured a few hours or days of peace, but the battle was far from over. The war was just beginning, and the Santhals were determined to emerge victorious, regardless of the price.

14 July 1855
Early evening
Towards Ganpur Bazaar,
Near Katna Village

The rain pounded down on the Santhals as they huddled in their new camp, seeking shelter from the deluge. The drops hammered against the canvas of their tents and turned the ground beneath their feet to mud. But it wasn't just the rain they were trying to escape. The memory of their recent losses haunted them, and they feared the watchful eyes of the British Army had been the reason behind their losses. They knew that if they remained in their old camp, the British would return with a greater force, find them and use their formidable weapons to crush their rebellion. So, they made the difficult decision to abandon their shelter in Katna village and venture out in search of a safer place to hide.

As the Santhals ventured into the dense jungle, their hearts beat with both fear and determination. The first group, led by the brave Chand, knew the importance of rallying reinforcements for Ganpur Bazaar.

'Remember, we are not just fighting for ourselves, but for all our people,' Chand reminded the group as they set out on their mission to rally the reinforcements for Ganpur Bazaar.

They rushed through the jungle, their feet pounding against the damp earth, their breaths ragged with exertion. They were the first line of defense against the British soldiers, and they would do whatever it would take to protect their people and their cause.

Meanwhile, the second group was being led by Bhairab, who kept on cautioning them to be wary of any British soldier who might be patrolling the area. 'Stay alert and keep your weapons at the ready,' he warned. The group moved carefully, aware of the danger that lurked around every corner. They kept a sharp lookout for any signs of the British soldiers, their ears tuned to the slightest sound that could give them away. They were the eyes and ears of the Santhal rebellion, and they would not let their guard down.

The third group, led by the fierce Phulo, had the daunting task of infiltrating the nearby Ganpur Bazaar. They knew that the bazaar was a haven for wealthy moneylenders, and they needed to procure the much-needed resources to support their cause. But they also knew that danger awaited them in the form of dikus and zamindars, who would stop at nothing to protect their own selfish interests.

As they neared Ganpur Bazaar, the Santhals grew more vigilant, knowing that their presence would not go unnoticed for long. The dikus and zamindars who controlled the town would not take kindly to their intrusion. The Santhals readied themselves for a fight, determined to do whatever it would take to secure the resources they needed for their survival.

With a concrete plan to bring Ganpur Bazaar under their

control, Kanhu had a bold idea: 'Why don't we take control of another bazaar? Let us control all the nearby bazaars and dominate the flow of money.'

The Santhals agreed to Kanhu's proposal, and they set their sights on the bazaar in Burhait. With their newfound confidence and success, they charged forward, eager to claim their next victory. But as they journeyed deeper into the jungle, they couldn't shake the feeling that they were being watched. The British Army was closing in, and the Santhals knew that their next battle would be the toughest one.

17 July 1855
Late morning
Burhait Baazar, Bhagalpur

Kanhu's and Chand's eyes widened in terror as they peered into the distance. They saw the approaching horde, a vast multitude of soldiers on foot and horseback, their numbers seeming to stretch beyond the horizon. The thud of the horses' hooves echoed through the forest, their breaths visible in the chilly air.

The Santhals had been on the move for weeks, their weary bodies pushed to the limit as they fought against the British oppression. They had taken over many areas, including Burhait Bazaar. Now, they knew they needed to rest and regroup. They set up a small camp on the outskirts of the bazaar, leaving only a minimum force to keep watch over the area.

Kanhu and Chand sat together near a campfire, their tired eyes scanning the forest for any signs of danger. They could hear the sound of the raindrops hitting the leaves above them.

'We need to keep moving,' Kanhu said, breaking the silence between them. 'We can't stay in one place for too long.'

Chand nodded in agreement. 'We need to be on the move to avoid the British soldiers. But we can't keep pushing ourselves like this. Our men need rest and time to recover.'

As they spoke, a messenger arrived with news of the approaching British Army. Kanhu and Chand realized the magnitude of the danger. They knew they needed to move quickly and quietly to avoid detection.

The Santhals broke camp and moved deeper into the forest, their wounded carried on their backs. They needed to find a place to rest and recover, but with the British Army on their heels, they knew it wouldn't be easy. Gentle rain continued to pour down on them as they moved, their tired bodies struggling to keep up the pace.

Chand's voice quivered as he whispered, 'There are so many of them, and I'm so tired.' But before he could shed a tear, the British Cavalry crashed into their village.

The ground beneath them shook as Kanhu's horn blared a warning and the Santhals scattered, following him through the dense trees. Bullets whizzed past them, zipping through the air and splintering the trees around them.

'Keep moving!' Kanhu shouted over the chaos. 'We can't let them catch us!'

Running in silence, they dodged trees and tried to stay low to the ground. Chand shouted, 'Get low and stay down!' as the sound of gunfire echoed through the forest. The deafening roar of the bullets and the crackling of the trees reverberated through the forest.

The Santhals hit the ground, their faces pressed into the dirt, hands covering their heads, trying not to dwell on the loss of their homes and loved ones. The smell of smoke and gunpowder hung in the air, the acrid smell filling their nostrils.

As the British claimed Burhait Bazaar, those who were left behind were captured and killed in a brutal show of force. The Santhal brothers and sisters lay motionless on the ground, their blood staining the earth. Kanhu and Chand survived, but their hearts were heavy as they thought of their fallen comrades and the uncertain future that lay ahead.

A couple of days later, Sido's heart sank with the arrival of a piece of news. He could hear the ominous rumble of the British soldiers approaching like a swarm of locusts. Everywhere they went, they left death and destruction in their wake. The Santhals had fought valiantly, but their numbers were dwindling and they were losing ground. Sido couldn't help but wonder, 'How many more of such troops can the British possibly have?'

As he pored over the oral reports, he noted the names of the enemy officers with a sense of foreboding. Captain Sherwill, Lieutenant Gordon and Lieutenant Rubee seemed to be at the forefront of every attack, and the Santhals were yet to find a way to stop them. Sido's mind raced as he wondered where these seemingly endless waves of soldiers were coming from. *Are the British soldiers coming from Kalikata?*

Sido wished they would just disappear, evaporate into thin air like the cold night. But the soldiers kept coming, like a never-ending tide, destroying anything and everything in their path. Sido could hardly bear to look at the devastation all around him. Homes had been burnt to the ground, and the once-beautiful land was now dark with smoke and ash. The distant cries of the wounded and dying echoed through the air. The British had caused immense destruction, and it seemed like they were revelling in their power.

It was clear that their enemy was determined to wipe out the Santhals once and for all. They attacked villages, even those that had not openly supported the rebellion, spreading the Santhal army thin. It was becoming a cruel joke, with the British treating the Santhals with even greater disdain than before.

After multiple losses of people, resources and land, the Santhals retreated to the forests, seeking refuge and a new plan. The forest welcomed them with open arms, offering a temporary sanctuary. They knew they needed to regroup and come up with a better strategy if they were to have any hope of surviving. The Santhals worked in silence, knowing that their next move would be critical in their fight for freedom.

Early August, 1855
Morning
Near Bhagalpur

The new commissioner, A.C. Bidwell, sat in his office near Bhagalpur with his officers, poring over maps and reports from the field. They had a daunting task ahead of them: to suppress the ongoing rebellion of the Santhals, who had been wreaking havoc in the forests for months. He was appointed as a special commissioner to suppress the rebellion.

Bidwell leaned forward, looking at his officers with a sense of urgency. 'Tell me, what is the situation on the ground?'

Captain Sherwill spoke up, 'The Santhals have lost many battles and villages, and their morale is low. But, Sir, we must be careful. They are hiding in the jungles, and they know the land better than us.'

Lieutenant Gordon added, 'They are also fighting for their homes and families. We cannot underestimate the Santhals and their determination.'

Bidwell nodded, 'I understand your concern, but we cannot let them continue their rebellion. We must send a message for them to surrender. If they don't, we will take necessary action.'

To that, Captain Sherwill said, 'We have an advantage in

firepower. They are not trained soldiers, and we have proper defences. We can make sure this ends in our favour.'

But Bidwell knew it wouldn't be that simple. The fear being experienced by the Santhals was palpable. They had lost their homes and were fighting for their survival. He said, 'We must use their fear to our advantage, but we must be cautious not to cause unnecessary bloodshed. We cannot afford to make mistakes.'

Bidwell was intelligent and shrewd. He knew that the situation was delicate and required a cautious approach. Bidwell was a man who believed in power and control, and he knew that the only way to maintain that control was to be strategic and cunning.

As he spoke to his officers, he made sure to emphasize that fear was a powerful motivator and that it could be used to manipulate the situation to their advantage. However, he also knew that any unnecessary violence could turn the Santhals against them for the long term and as a result, they would have fewer people to hire for working on the lands.

As the officers continued their discussion, Bidwell's mind raced with possibilities. The situation would need to be handled in a nuanced manner. He thought about the option of buying time, knowing that it would allow them to surround the Santhals and capture or kill their key leaders without causing unnecessary bloodshed.

As the commissioner and his officers continued to discuss their plan of action, Bidwell also made sure to mention the possibility of a peace call. 'We must consider all options. If there is a way to end this without further violence, we must adopt it. We cannot let this rebellion continue to ravage the land and harm innocent people.' His words were met with nods of agreement from his officers, who knew that a peaceful resolution would be preferable to a long and drawn-out conflict.

Captain Sherwill spoke up again, 'Sir, if we do offer a peace call, what terms should we offer?'

Bidwell paused, considering the question. 'We must offer them some deal that looks fair but protects our interests more.'

Lieutenant Gordon added, 'We could offer them the option to return to their homes, giving them temporary amnesty and allowing them to list their grievances.'

Bidwell nodded, 'That is a good start. We must also offer them a chance to rebuild and develop their villages and get education facilities for their children. We will educate their children in our ways of life. We will convert them one by one.' His officers nodded in agreement, impressed by Bidwell's vision for a peaceful future.

Bidwell knew that such resolution would not only end the immediate conflict but would also be crucial for the long-term stability of the region.

No farmer, no economy, he thought.

After having the discussion, the officers left the room, determined to carry out their mission with caution and strategic thinking, knowing that a peaceful resolution was within reach.

Early August, 1855
Afternoon
Oporbandha Village

Kanhu and Sido crouched in the thick of the jungle, surrounded by towering trees that whispered in the wind. The earth beneath their feet was cool and damp, a comforting presence against their soles. Moments like these made them feel alive and connected to the land that they were fighting for. Kanhu broke the stillness with a question that had been weighing on his mind.

'Why do you think the British have offered us a peace call?' he asked his brother, his eyes searching for answers.

Sido scoffed, 'They have no such intention. They want us to surrender, so that they can have their way with us.'

Kanhu nodded thoughtfully. 'That could be true, but there might be another reason. What if they are afraid of losing and want to avoid further bloodshed?'

Sido shook his head, 'You're too naive, brother. The British are not weak. They want to keep us alive, so we can continue to work for them. Dead rebels cannot harvest their crops, build their roads or make their baskets.'

A sense of understanding dawned on Kanhu. 'I see. So they

need us alive to do their dirty work. But we will not surrender. We will fight until the end and let the earth embrace us when we fall.'

Sido nodded in agreement. 'We will not give them the satisfaction they are looking for. We will fight till our last breath.'

With renewed determination, the brothers discussed tactics and headed back to their respective camps. Their families were waiting for them, and they knew that they had to protect them at all costs. The jungle may have been their home, but it was also a dangerous place. They had to be ready for whatever the British had planned next.

As the evening settled over the camp, Mala sat with her children, trying to keep them occupied as they waited for Sido's return. She couldn't help but worry about what he was facing out there in the jungle. She knew that he was a brave man and a skilled fighter, but the uncertainty of the battles weighed heavily on her mind. She had grown accustomed to the constant fear of the British Army and their merciless tactics, but that didn't make it any easier to bear.

As the hours passed, her worry grew to a fever pitch, and she found herself pacing back and forth in front of the small hut they called home. She wondered if Sido was safe and if he would return to them. As she anxiously scanned the darkness, she finally saw her husband's form emerging from the shadows.

Overcome with emotion, she ran towards him and threw her arms around him, tears streaming down her face. Sido gently pulled her back, searching her tear-streaked face for an explanation. Mala could barely speak, her throat tight with emotion. Finally, she managed to utter, 'I was so worried about you. Are you alright?'

Sido smiled and stroked her hair, 'I am fine, Mala. Don't worry about me.' However, Mala couldn't help but worry. Sido was fighting for their people's freedom, and that meant he was constantly putting himself in danger. She didn't know how much longer she could bear the uncertainty of their lives, but she knew that they had to keep fighting for their future.

Mala struggled to find the right words, her fear for Sido and the future of their people being a constant source of worry for her. 'I'm worried about what will happen to us,' she finally managed to say.

Sido's surprise was palpable. 'What do you mean?'

'I don't want to lose you,' she said. 'The British will kill you if you keep rebelling against them.'

Sido's expression hardened. 'I cannot abandon my clan,' he said firmly. 'Others can lead, but I cannot leave them, not after all that we've sacrificed.'

Mala's face crumpled with emotion, and she pleaded with him. 'But I love you, Sido,' she said. 'I cannot bear to lose you.'

Sido held her close, his voice low and reassuring. 'I will be safe,' he promised. 'We will fight together and we will win.'

In spite of his assurances, Mala couldn't shake the feeling of dread. 'What if we lose?' she asked, her voice trembling.

Sido's face grew fierce. 'We will not lose,' he said. 'The Santhals have always fought back and we will continue to do so. We are making history. Stories will be told about us.'

Mala's determination grew, and she knew that she could not

stand by and watch from the sidelines. 'I want to fight with you,' she said, her voice firm.

Sido hesitated, 'Think it over,' he said. 'It is not an easy path, and it is not without risk.'

But Mala was resolute. 'I am determined to fight for our people,' she said. 'I will not let fear hold me back.'

And so, with her husband by her side, Mala joined the front lines, determined to fight for the freedom of their land. Phulo and Jano, fierce warriors like their brothers, led the charge, and together, the Murmu clan fought with all their might to protect their people and their future.

There were some minor skirmishes, and every time the police tried to arrest the leaders of the clan, the warriors fought to save them. Many of them lost their lives, but their spirit never wavered. They became famous across the Santhal land, and many other tribes joined them to fight against the oppression of landlords and the British.

One late afternoon, Sido and Mala were alone, far from the camp. Sido was worried about the cut near his wife's abdomen after being injured in a minor skirmish. 'I should have stopped you from joining the battle,' he said.

Taking his hand in hers, Mala said in an reassuring way, 'I had a dream, Sido.'

'A dream?' he enquired, confused.

Mala nodded. 'I saw us in a battle, with burning trees all around us.'

Sido's eyes widened. 'What happened to us in the dream?'

'We both died together,' she answered, looking at the sky

above that was beginning to growl with thunder.

'I should never have let you join the clan,' he repeated, blaming himself.

Mala silenced him with a finger on his lips. 'You mean everything to me, Sido. Even if I die, I will die happy knowing that we are together,' she said, gazing into his eyes.

Suddenly, the thunder grew louder, and Mala refused to leave for shelter. She wanted to experience the thrill of the approaching storm, raindrops splashing onto her skin. Sido eventually joined her, and they both laughed and danced, getting soaked. The sound of thunder echoed like a warning of the struggles to come, but they were not afraid. They knew their love was stronger than any storm, and that no matter what, they would always be together.

Mid-August, 1855
Commissioner Office of Behrampur

Many miles away, Commissioner A.C. Bidwell was gazing out of the window of his office, past the pastures below. It had been a few days since the Santhals had attacked. The question was what would their response be.

He was sure they were carefully considering their decision, but the fact that they were thinking was a good sign. Bidwell was confident that the Santhals would soon yield.

Incompetence would not be tolerated, so Bidwell had ensured that all armed troops were ready and waiting for any signs of the Santhals' return. They would not be caught off guard.

Suddenly, the door swung open and a man stormed into Bidwell's office. 'Sir, they have attacked another bazaar. Our local sympathizers have been wiped out!'

Bidwell's eyebrows furrowed in confusion. *Have they lost their minds?* 'How many of them were there? Weren't our troops in that village?'

'Yes, Sir, but they couldn't stop them. They were decimated, and the village was burnt to the ground. Everything, even the police station is gone.'

Bidwell couldn't believe it. Looking at the scale of the

destruction, he realized there must have been a large number of Santhals. Regardless, they needed to act quickly. The Santhals seemed to have decided that there would be no more mercy.

'Call Captain Sherwill!' Bidwell ordered.

The battle intensified, and Bidwell was not pleased with the progress. Although the Santhals were poorly equipped, they made up for it with their determination and guerrilla tactics.

The British had never seen anything like it. Even when they fired their guns, the Santhals never ran. With the dense forest all around, the British could not get a clear line of fire.

The generals realized that to defeat the enemy, they must understand them first. They used locals to guide them through the forests, avoiding pitfalls. However, it made little difference. The Santhals rampaged through Dumka, taking down villages with ease.

Bidwell needed to act quickly or the Santhals would continue with the destruction.

Fighting a war is like playing chess. To win, each move must be carefully considered. The same was true in real life. The British army needed an excellent strategy to win the war.

We will capture Sido. There will be people who will want to betray him, and our spies will identify them. We just need to know who not to trust.

Mid-August, 1855
Near Sangrampur
Rajmahal Hills

The night sky was bathed in the silvery glow of the full moon. Dust danced across the open grasslands. The tall blades of grass swayed in the wind, while a gentle drizzle descended upon the earth, filling the air with the fragrance of damp soil.

It was said that history was written by the victors, but on this night, over a thousand sons and daughters of the Santhal land had gathered to create history, not for their sake, but for their future generations and for the preservation of their way of life.

Standing tall with a muscular frame, Sido carried himself with a commanding presence. A quiver full of arrows was slung across his chest, and a dhoti was tightly wrapped around his legs. In his hands, he held a bow, ready to battle what lay ahead.

Sido breathed in the scent of the wet soil, closing his eyes briefly. *My land*, he thought, feeling the aroma of the earth rise within his soul. With close to forty years of experience, Sido knew that what he was about to do would inspire the younger generations to fight for their family and tribe.

As Sido's mind wandered, he thought of his younger,

short-tempered brother, Kanhu. While Sido was on the front lines, Kanhu was positioned a few kilometres away, surrounded by a few hundred warriors and his two younger brothers, Chand and Bhairab. The three younger brothers were waiting for a signal from Sido to advance into battle.

Sido and his forces were stationed atop Rajmahal Hills, numbering over a thousand determined Santhal warriors. The hill was a mixture of rocks and short shrubs, with steep inclines in some places that would make it difficult for the British army to ascend. This gave the Santhals a significant tactical advantage, with their warriors positioned at the top, ready to unleash a hail of arrows. Meanwhile, other guerrilla forces were hidden, waiting to attack the British army from the flanks once the battle began. It was a matter of who would make the first move.

At the front of the British army were dozens of elephants, carrying flags and banners. Behind them, mounted cavalries marched, each man equipped with a rifle and sword. The army was now a mix of British soldiers and their benefactors, like the Nawab's army, with the crunch of their boots echoing as they advanced. But as they reached the hill and saw the hundreds of Santhal warriors waiting for them, they knew that this would not be an easy battle. These benefactors, while similar in appearance to the Santhals, were vastly different in their beliefs and actions. They were subservient in nature, with their gods being power and money rather than nature.

'They're here now, Sido,' said Bhagna.

'Yes, Bhagna,' replied Sido. 'And this is a battle we will win.'

'With you at the helm, we're sure to win,' Bhagna added.

Bhagna was a man of average height with a lean build. His skin was tanned from years spent in the sun, and his features were sharp, giving him an air of cunningness. His eyes were dark and piercing, always assessing the situation and sizing up those around him. Over the last few days, he had come close to Sido to gain his trust.

Sido and Bhagna embraced each other gently. Over the last few months, Bhagna had grown close to the Murmu brothers and was now a trusted friend of the family. The two friends parted ways, each heading to different parts of the hill to prepare for the impending attack or defence.

'They're coming,' said Sido. 'The British are going to attack. They won't hold back.'

The Santhals knew the hills and weather well, but the wind would make things more complicated. They needed their arrows to fly straight today. They knew that the fight would have to take place at close range at some point.

'Look, they're advancing,' one of the chiefs shouted to Sido. He nodded and instructed the messenger to relay the information to Bhagna that the attack had begun on their side of the hill. The messenger whistled loudly. Then there came a message that the enemy was also marching from the other side of the hill.

'Start the drumbeats,' said Sido.

A few Santhals moved forward, armed with small, hand-held drums made of animal leather and wooden bodies.

The East India Company Cavalry unit was in position, facing the open ground, which was almost entirely dark except for the faint moonlight. In the moonlight, they could see a red-haired officer on horseback. It was Major Vincent Jervis.

He had been absent throughout all the battles and skirmishes that had taken place. It was a question that was on everyone's mind—where had he been?

There were rumours doing the rounds among the soldiers, with some claiming that he was injured or had been taken captive by the enemy, while others whispered that he had deserted his unit. The truth, however, was far more complicated than any of them could have imagined.

Vincent had been facing a moral dilemma. He was torn between the demands of the empire and sympathy for Mina's people. As he had watched the violence and bloodshed unfold, he had begun to question the righteousness of the Company's actions. He had then been transferred to the Company headquarters in Kalikata.

For days, he had grappled with his thoughts and struggled to reconcile his loyalty to the Company with his own sense of right and wrong. It was only after much soul-searching that he had come to a decision—he would stand by the British Empire. When he saw his friends and fellow officers get slaughtered, he requested his commander to send him to the frontlines.

Now, as he sat atop his horse, facing the open ground in front of him, he knew that the moment of reckoning had come. The fate of the rebellion and the lives of countless people hung in the balance. Vincent could feel the weight of his decision bearing down on him, but he was firm. He would do what was right for the Queen, his country and Lord.

The battle picked up momentum.

'Men!' Vincent cried out. 'Charge forward!'

The British cavalry advanced, riding to the sound of the drums. Their horses galloped, kicking up dust into the night sky. Vincent knew that these tribals were ready to die, but he also knew that history would remember them as the victors. The first war for independence in Bharat was about to begin.

That was when the Santhal army struck, with their volley of arrows streaming down like vicious rainfall. The forward troops were ordered to step back to avoid being shot by the arrows. Sido made note of that and asked to stop the firing. *No need to waste the arrows. What will they do now? They might bring their gunners ahead to fire bullets. The order for firing is going to be given any moment now. Let us move back and see what range they have.*

'Move back! Move back!' he shouted.

The Santhals took a few steps back, waiting to see what the enemy would do next.

'Fire! Fire!' shouted the mounted officers.

There were surprisingly few flashes, and the light smoke soon cleared. The sepoys looked at each other confused.

The Santhals saw from above. Shots had been fired from hundreds of guns, but no bullet hit them. The tribals started to laugh, thinking the enemy was just trying to scare them.

'Look, they are reloading their guns. Maybe this time we will not be so lucky.'

The sound of gunfire echoed across the battlefield as the mounted officers gave the firing order again. The sepoys were advancing. The tension was palpable. The British soldiers were on edge, knowing that any moment could be their last. But they had to remain focussed, keep their aim steady and follow orders.

The second round of shots rang out, and the smoke started to clear. The sepoys began checking their guns, frantically trying to reload.

'It's not firing,' one of them shouted. The British soldiers started moving helter-skelter. There was chaos.

Sido and other Santhal leaders scanned the situation from the hilltop. They were excited.

'Look again. No bullet hit us, their guns are not firing. We will charge now and finish them off.'

The tribal leaders readied their men for the charge.

'Wait! Look there…on that hill, behind the trees. Something is moving,' Sido said, pointing towards a faraway hill.

All Santhals looked in that direction, and they could see something big being moved from one place to another behind the tree line.

'What is it?' asked one of the leaders.

There was a whistling sound—a new command. It was coming from Bhagna. He appeared at a distance and signalled towards Sido's section of the army.

Attack now, as Thakur has blessed us.

'Bhagna is saying our Lord Thakur has blessed us. And he has commanded his side to attack.' Sido was told by one of the messengers.

'What do we do?' one of the tribal commanders asked Sido.

A lightning bolt hit the ground. The British frontline was in disarray. The sky grew darker. A low rumble started building up in the distance.

SIDO KANHU

It is true that Thakur is blessing us with the lightning strike? Sido wondered.

Everyone waited patiently till there was another whistling sound. Sido and his group of commanders turned towards Bhagna to check for any signals.

Bhagna has ordered the troops to move down. He did not wait for my command. Sido could see the Santhals warriors from Bhagna's army rushing down the hill.

'We will go together. We will either win together or die together,' Sido shouted, raising his sword towards the British front line.

'Now?' one of the leaders asked.

'Yes, now. Let the battle begin,' Sido replied.

He ran down towards the plains, closely followed by the other Santhals. He turned around and looked at the ten boys, all in their teens, running with him, all ready to fight.

'Come here, guys,' he shouted. 'Wait until I give orders.' Before turning back to face the front, he added, 'Don't forget, our goal is victory.'

A moment later, they heard another rumbling sound. The next second, a cannon fired. The earth shook violently and everyone felt the tremors. They all stood still, looking up at the heavens as the smoke went up in the sky. When the smoke cleared, they saw a terrifying sight—the first glimpse of the British army. Thousands of soldiers lined both sides of the broken, dusty road leading to the hill. Horses galloped along the muddy path carrying soldiers, whose swords glistened in the rain. Officers on horseback wearing colourful uniforms rode amongst them. At least twenty cannons fired simultaneously, sending plumes of smoke high into the sky. Between the plumes were dozens of other artillery pieces firing continuously.

The Santhals didn't stop. They ran towards the frontline of the British sepoys. The latter were surprised by the speed at which the Santhals were approaching. The frontline of riflemen quickly retreated, but it wasn't over yet. A second and third line of sepoys with rifles, along with British officers on horses, ran towards the Santhals and fired their guns in a synchronized chorus of blasts.

Shots were fired and a few Santhals were hit, but the rest still charged forward. Sido quickly realized what had happened. *The bullets are hitting us now. Earlier, they had used dummy bullets.*

On the run, Sido commanded his fellow comrades to spread out, so that the bullets would instead hit the large tree trunks and bushes, and not them. The Santhals, meanwhile, slipped in between large rocks, looking for cover. From their hiding places, they managed to attack the sepoys and British officers on horses with a series of arrows. After the first wave of arrows and hand-to-hand combat, more sepoys of the British army fell.

Sido saw someone, camouflaged in the field. *It's Kanhu. He broke ranks to support me. Where the hell is Bhagna's group? They should have joined us here. Are they all dead?*

Blood dripped from their wounds as Kanhu led his group against the sepoys. Surrounded by the Santhals, the sepoys struggled to form a shooting range to fire. Sido and some others snuck in and fought them with swords, disrupting their fire flow.

Sido noted that many of the soldiers deployed by the British looked like them, with most of them speaking the same language as the Santhals. There were even instances where they could have dined together. The East India Company was always in need of new recruits to bolster their ranks. They looked for able-bodied men who could fight and were willing to join them in their cause. They had found many of them in the local Indian population. These men were attracted to the steady pay and other benefits offered by the Company, and many of them had personal reasons to fight for the British. But now they were entangled in conflict. The battle intensified, more bullets were fired and hand-to-hand combat became difficult as the firing was now coming from a distance.

Sido's comrades were being hit and many fell. The sepoys lost their men, too. However, the number of wounded and dead on the Santhal side was higher.

Sido wanted to give it another try. *One more push.*

'Santhals...Hul, Hul, Hul,' cried out Sido.

The Santhals started shouting in unison, following their leader.

'Hul!'

'Hul!'

'Hul!'

The Santhals charged towards the enemy, this time in smaller groups, to minimize any negative impact in the face of an attack by the British.

I need a bow. Sido raced on his bare feet to grab a bow that belonged to a fallen Santal. In one swift motion, he picked it up, rolled over and fired three arrows towards the fast-approaching cavalry, each hitting a British officer in the neck or chest, causing them to fall. The Santhals rushed to the fallen officers and plunged their swords into them, causing bloodstreams to gush from their mouths.

Shirtless and sweating, Sido raised his bow as the men cheered uproariously, feeling that the blessings of their ancestors were upon them. With more turns like this, they could conquer the British. The fierce battle raged on for a few more minutes, but the Santhals' numbers dwindled. They had been lured into the attack, thinking the British army's guns were not working, but it was a trick to draw them out in the open.

Sido looked around and saw more deaths. His brother Chand was surrounded by five sepoys and was fighting alone. One of the sepoys pierced a sword into Chand's waist, causing him to scream and call out for Thakur. Sido cried out loud and ran towards his brother.

I have only one arrow left. I have to save Chand, he thought.

Chand fell, but not before swinging his sword and decapitating two of the sepoys. The remaining sepoys were swinging their swords towards Chand when one was hit by an arrow. The other ran away in fear. The last sepoy felt pain in his chest and died instantly as Sido, with sheer brute force, plunged the blunt end of the bow into his chest. Sido lifted Chand and looked at him, but Chand was unconscious and wounded.

'No! I promised Mother I would take care of you until my death, and I am still breathing,' Sido said.

Sido called for a retreat, and all the Santhals began their journey back towards the jungle. They knew they could not win the battle that day. They had been tricked, and not all their forces had come together as planned. Sido hoped that the next day would bring with it the promise of a counterattack.

Sido quickly instructed Kanhu to make medical arrangements for the hundreds of injured Santhals. Sadly, some succumbed after suffering from serious injuries.

Bhagna's group met with Sido's. Though Sido was irritated at Bhagna for not being able to come down in time for the attack, Bhagna's group later aided them during their retreat. They had also acquired many guns, giving the Santhals at least a hundred rifles to use in the future.

Sido observed the changes taking place around him. His people were standing up to fight for their rights and he was proud, but his mind was filled with turbulent thoughts. Many had died, and many more would as they continued to fight. Death was inevitable, but there was no way he would let their children live with the possibility of a future that was bleak. The Santhals had been considered slaves, but now they had decided to be masters of their own destinies.

They knew they would lose their chance if they allowed the British to win or gain complete control. They couldn't step back now. They needed to attack the British such that their economic power would be destroyed—by targeting their bazaars, zamindars and moneylenders. The foreigners in their land wouldn't win this war for their British masters.

Therefore, Sido ordered a change of strategy. Instead of direct attacks, they would switch back to guerrilla warfare and cut off supply routes.

A week passed. Soon, a target was decided. The first target was the Bhognadih Bazaar, which was burnt down completely, and the moneylenders were killed.

After a few days, Sido gathered his best fighters and marched into Pirpainti, a crucial hub for British activity. He issued two orders. First, there would be five more attacks at various locations, with not more than a hundred Santhals participating in each attack. The objective was straightforward: Kill all sympathizers, but spare a few, so they could reach their British superiors and convey their message. The other order was for smaller groups of around thirty Santhals to move closer to smaller villages and checkpoints, making themselves visible, but refraining from attacks. Fifteen such groups were formed and dispersed. The order was straightforward: Show yourself but don't attack; if challenged, retreat into the forests; draw the British into the jungles and then ambush them.

Once both orders were carried out, the next phase of the attack would begin. In Pirpainti, the local police and moneylenders were shocked as they never expected an attack from the Santhals. The small town was being defended with a structure that included machine guns and a small contingent of around fifty cavalries led by a British officer. However, the town was caught off guard as the Santhals approached. The police force and moneylenders gathered their guns, hoping to fend off the attackers, but Chand and Bhairab, who were in charge of the assault, had already infiltrated the town.

During the skirmish, the Santhals killed most of the British sympathizers and, according to their plan, allowed a few to escape. These few reached out to the British officers of higher ranks, who were stationed at base camps in different locations, and gave them the details of the attack. The news of multiple attacks on smaller villages and towns reached the British.

At the core base camp in Bhagalpur, the commissioners and the army leadership discussed the change in strategy used by the Santhals. A senior officer in the room asked, 'Are there any outsiders helping them?' The British concluded that the Santhals' tactics were accidental and that they were attempting to spread out the British forces.

The East India Company ordered Major Burroughs to reclaim the area and sent a detachment of three hundred men and about a hundred horses from the capital. Within two days, Burroughs and his detachment reached Pirpainti. He ordered a smaller detachment of four fully armed horsemen to move in different directions to search for the Santhals' trail. Seven detachments were sent with orders to return within two hours if they saw nothing. After about an hour, one of the detachments returned, reporting that they had located the Santhals.

A party of around fifty Santhals was seen walking around the jungle edge near lowly elevated grounds. Burroughs left fifty soldiers and ten horsemen in the town and moved towards the confirmed location of the Santhals. Two Santhals, perched on branches of trees, started making whistling noises. Bhairab and others heard the calls. The message was conveyed: 'Three hundred men, about fifty of them on horses over here. They are going to get the biggest surprise of their lives. Time to inform Chand.'

When Burroughs and his detachment reached the location, about thirty Santhals charged towards them. The battle began, and Burroughs ordered his men to spare no tribal groups. The mounted officers and foot soldiers advanced towards the Santhals.

Bhairab led the small battalion of Santhals, exposing themselves to the hill rangers.

'Just wait. They're almost here. Let them come closer to us,' said Bhairab. 'Now!'

The Santhals ran towards the British. They shot arrows, threw stones and turned around in less than a minute.

'Chase them,' shouted one of the officers.

Around three hundred British troops chased after the small Santhal force. They raised their matchlocks and fired, hitting a few Santhals. Despite getting injured, they got up, either on their own or with some help of their fellow warriors, and started running in a zig-zag pattern.

'What the hell are they doing?' one of the officers shouted to Burroughs. The latter frowned but continued to lead his troops. He slowed down along with a few officers as the elevation decreased. He quickly looked to both sides.

'The elevation is decreasing from three sides, and we're following them. It's a trap,' he realized.

The British soldiers and sepoys momentarily halted as they saw the Santhals attacking them from the left and right flanks. Hundreds of Santhals crouched on either side of the elevated grounds, and more were hiding on the small hills.

Suddenly, there were sounds of gunshots. The sepoys realized that the arms were their own and, in fact, the same ones snatched by the Santhals in the earlier combat. As the sepoys and their British masters approached, the Santhals moved swiftly to engage them. They succeeded in surrounding their enemy.

With guns as well as arrows, now the Santhals could cover a longer range in the battlefield. Many sepoys fell. The Santhals tore through the sepoys and British officers, leaving them confused and gasping for relief.

The sepoys soon lost their spirit, as what drove them was not passion but greed for gold and silver coins. In contrast, the Santhals were not fighting for wealth. They were fighting to provide food for their children and to stake their claim on their homeland.

Sido charged into the battle, his sword bringing down multiple sepoys. A bullet from Burroughs struck him in the thigh, but he continued fighting. Other Santhals came to his aid, and Bhagna raced ahead to protect Sido, with his body acting as a shield. Bhagna attempted to attack Burroughs, but the latter turned his horse and retreated. In spite of his injury, Sido continued to fight as night fell.

The windy weather and rustling leaves mixed with the distant screams of fallen soldiers. The Santhals had an advantage in the dim light, but they still chose to show mercy to their enemies by not using their typical poison-laced arrows, which they normally used while hunting animals. Santhals believed that a fellow human should be spared dishonour at his hour of death.

The British force rapidly decreased in number, and only a few mounted officers, including Burroughs, managed to escape. The Santhals did not pursue them and instead let out a loud cry of victory as the retreating army galloped into the sunset.

News of the battle spread, following which many more Santhals eagerly joined Sido's army. The rebels' morale remained high. They succeeded in defeating a significant portion of the British army. Sido was taken away from the frontlines to Bhagna's village as he needed to be attended to.

For the British, it was a dark day. They quickly requested reinforcements and there were talks of implementing martial law. The Santhals, meanwhile, were working on enforcing their own laws, as the land was theirs.

Mid-August, 1855
Bhognadih

The Santhals' success story so far had been remarkable. However, as seen in any battle, cases of injured comrades and sepoys were increasing. Sido was aware that the British considered this fight a disgrace and felt that they shouldn't be struggling to defeat the Santhals. This only served to boost the morale of Sido's troops, who were amazed that they could go head-to-head with the British and emerge victorious.

After partially recovering, Sido and his brothers, along with a few hundred Santhals, launched another raid in Tappa Belpatta of the Bhagalpur district. They managed to burn the police station and the houses of zamindars, but Sido was injured again. This time too, he was shot in the thigh. He moved back to Bhagna's village to recuperate, but his brothers advised him to rest and fully recover before rejoining the fight. Sido quickly learnt that winning could inspire praise and love just as much as envy and jealousy.

Meanwhile, Bhagna provided medical care and a secluded place for Sido to rest and recover. Sido's routine included taking rest, walking along the riverside, taking medicines on time and returning to the hut by the evening. After a few days, he started feeling better. One evening, while resting by the riverside, his brothers paid him a visit and shared more news of their victories. Sido was pleased to see that their fight had not stopped in his absence.

Bhagna arrived with a mixture of herbs and fresh goat milk for Sido. As usual, Sido complained about the bitter taste, but Bhagna insisted that it was sweet. He eventually drank the entire mixture, and after a few moments, Bhagna and he walked back to the hut. Suddenly, Sido became drowsy and stumbled. Bhagna helped him inside and put him to bed.

As he fell asleep, Bhagna packed his belongings into a small bag and placed it next to the bed. After coming out from the hut, Bhagna saw a small boat coming towards the shore of the river. There were men with rifles in the boat. He quietly walked away from the hut, leaving Sido behind in an unconscious state.

Mid-August, 1855
Bhognadih and Panchkathia

Sido couldn't believe he had fallen for Bhagna's deceit. He lay on the ground in Bhagna's dark hut in Bhognadih, feeling the pain from his previous battles fade. With all the medical care he had provided, Bhagna had seemed like a godsend. It was only now that Sido had come to realize the truth: He had been drugged, and now he was being dragged out of the hut by a group of unknown men as he was struggling to regain complete consciousness. Sido tried to resist, but his body was numb and his mind was foggy from the drink Bhagna had brought for him.

Sido's eyes fluttered open, and he saw that he was surrounded by British soldiers. Panic set in as he realized that he had been captured. The soldiers bound his wrists tightly, and Sido knew that the noose of his execution was already being prepared. He was helpless and his fate was sealed.

The soldiers took him to Bhognadih village, where he was thrown into a cold, dark prison cell. Sido's mind raced with thoughts of how he could have been so careless, so foolish. He was a leader, a warrior, but now he was a captive. The cell was small and damp, and the small opening in the ceiling was the only source of light.

I should have known and I should have taken precautions. They are always coming for me... I am the leader of this rebellion.

Sido's chest heaved with pain, his body bruised and battered from the beatings he had endured from his captors. He gritted his teeth, determined not to show any weakness in front of his enemies. But the dingy cell in which he was imprisoned was a constant reminder of his powerlessness. The thudding footsteps of the British soldiers and their uniforms stained with the blood of his people made Sido feel nauseated.

He sat in the back of the cell, his eyes fixed on the opposite wall, trying to control his breathing, but the throbbing pain made it difficult to do so. The other captives, both Santhals as well as others, were in no better shape—some tied up and others not, all of them bloodied, beaten and bruised, just like Sido.

Even during times of peace, the British had oppressed the Santhal people in subtle ways, and Sido wondered if it was better to endure the pain slowly or experience it swiftly and directly, the way he was experiencing it right now. He knew that death was inevitable, but he preferred a physical death to a spiritual one.

As a leader, he knew that the fear and uncertainty his tribesmen were experiencing was palpable. They wondered if their sacrifices meant anything in a time like this. But he had to be strong, he had to represent a united front and prove that their hope was not in vain.

'Listen to me, my fellow Santhals,' Sido addressed the other captives. The sepoys in charge of security had beaten him up, but he continued to raise his voice. 'Know this and understand this: I am fine. Don't look at my injuries and despair. I've never been better.'

One of the men replied, 'They won't break us. Your brother will come to free us. He'll crush them, and their blood will bless the trees of our land.'

The cell echoed with cheers, and Sido allowed himself a brief smile. But suddenly, the door slammed open and a man stepped inside. It was another officer, Major Shuckburgh.

Shuckburgh's boots echoed against the tiled floor, growing louder as he approached Sido. 'Where is Kanhu?' he demanded, his voice carrying a sense of urgency.

Sido said, 'If you expect me to reveal the location of our camps and people, you are wasting your time.'

Shuckburgh smirked and stooped before Sido. 'You have a lot of arrogance to assume you'll win this war.'

'No, you're just a fool,' Sido replied. 'We were never trying to win the war. Our aim was to win our freedom. It's not about defeating you; it is about preserving our land. You may take my life, but it won't matter because we will reclaim our land by the end.'

Shuckburgh chuckled at Sido's words. 'You're the real fool here. That land was never yours to begin with. Have you forgotten who your master is? We are! We gave you the right to that land. All you had to do was pay your dues and live your miserable lives in peace. But you became arrogant and thought there was more to life.'

Sido shrugged, 'Maybe you're right about that. Maybe you'll always be our masters, and we will always be the earth beneath your feet. That's understandable. I believe you're right. But you're also wrong because even though you are our masters, you do not own this land. We were here before you and we've made it clear that our spirit is not dead. You can rule with all your might, but we will always be here, just like our ancestors. Our children will be here just like their ancestors. The cycle will never end and you will never find peace in our land.'

Other prisoners around started shouting, 'Hul! Hul! Hul!'

Shuckburgh looked around him and noticed what Sido was talking about: Their spirit wasn't broken. He growled, 'Let's see how confident you will be when the hangman is choking you. Guards! Take him to Panchkathia where the courts will decide his future.'

They came, swept up Sido and took him out.

After a few hours, they reached Bhagalpur. There was a substantial presence of British troops there. It was like a small fortress, but they allowed the local population to move around. The natives in the area came out to witness Sido's downfall, along with that of his followers. He was soon put on trial. The British authorities had little interest in the due process, and the trial was a mere formality. Sido was quickly found guilty of leading the rebellion and sentenced to death by hanging. Shuckburgh watched with a sense of satisfaction. For him, the hanging acted as a clear message to the Santhals that the British power was absolute and that any resistance would be brutally crushed.

Sido was now in Panchkathia, chained and bound with iron and ropes. He was made to walk towards his death while all watched and spoke of what was about to happen. Only three days had passed since he had been captured. The news had spread, but it was too late to save him.

As the noose was placed around his neck, memories of his family members flashed in front of his eyes. He didn't want his life to end like this, but he put on a strong face and held his head up with pride, not wanting to appear as if he was begging for mercy. Sido tried to be strong even in his weakest moment. But the cold and hateful eyes of the British and their sympathizers weighed heavily on him.

Sido closed his eyes, trying to find some semblance of peace. Memories from his days as a slave to his rise as a leader flashed before his eyes. He smiled, thinking of the victories they had won together, the battles they had fought and overcome.

As the platform dropped from under his feet and he was released into the unknown, Sido shouted, 'Freedom always! Hul, Hul, Hul!' He wanted to let those around him know that he never gave in to despair, not even till his last breath. They could take his body, but they would never conquer the passion with which he fought.

For the British, Sido's death in Panchkathia was a message that anyone who continued to engage in war would meet the same fate as their leader. Sido's body dangled violently. His legs shook for a while and his neck cracked. He was Sido one moment ago, and now he was just a body without a voice. He was dead, but his memories would live as long as his name was spoken.

Early September, 1855
Bhognadih and Ganpur Bazaar

Mala sat alone in the darkness of her humble hut, her trembling hands obscuring her delicate features. As she struggled to come to terms with the harsh reality that her beloved husband was gone forever, tears streamed down her face, wetting her hands. It felt like a cruel nightmare from which she could not awaken, and her heart ached with sorrow.

Her mind raced with the memories of their past, the laughter, the love, the fights and the comfort. Mala couldn't help but wonder how she could ever hope to carry on without him. The enormity of her loss weighed heavy on her, crushing her chest and making it hard to breathe. She wished she could turn back time and change the course of events that led to Sido's tragic fate. She longed to tell him how much she loved him one last time, to hold him close and feel the warmth of his embrace.

But it was too late, and she knew she had to summon the strength to carry on for the sake of their children. Her grief was quickly overshadowed by her concern for the safety of her people and the continuation of the revolution that Sido had fought so hard for. She knew that the loss of their leader could weaken the movement and put them in even more danger.

SIDO KANHU

Her thoughts turned to Kanhu, the young warrior who had taken up Sido's mantle. She wondered if he was ready for the responsibility and if he could lead their people to victory. Mala prayed for his safety, hoping he would be guided by the wisdom of his predecessors.

Kanhu rose from his morning prayers with tears in his eyes, his heart heavy with grief. The news of his brother's hanging had spread like wildfire throughout the Santhals, stirring a dangerous mix of anger and frustration. Half the Santhals were consumed with rage, while the other half despaired, their hope and motivation stripped away. Kanhu knew that he had to act quickly to rally his people, to give them the courage to carry on through the dark times they were living in.

We must not surrender, Kanhu whispered to himself, his voice trembling with emotion. *We cannot let Sido's sacrifice go in vain.*

As the day wore on, Kanhu received news that Bhagna had been tracked down and killed by a group led by Chand, who himself was recovering from his injury. It was a small victory, but a victory nonetheless. Kanhu knew that it would lift the spirits of his people, even if only temporarily. But he also knew that there would always be more like Bhagna in future. To instill fear in the hearts of such followers, Kanhu ordered the execution of those who had supported Bhagna, showing no mercy.

Days later, more Santhals arrived at the village camp. Bhagna and his supporters' deaths had made one thing clear: The Santhals would not tolerate any form of betrayal. Those who remained loyal to the cause would now fight until the very end.

As Kanhu walked towards the meeting place in the village

camp, his eyes grew moist, a tear escaping down his cheek.

Do we need a new camp? Kanhu wondered as the current camp was filled with memories of their losses. He knew there was one more reason to fight now.

I need to avenge my leader, my brother, and continue to fight for Thakur.

Kanhu was determined to not let the revolution fail without a fight. As the British struggled to defeat Santhals, martial law was imposed over Bhagalpur, Murshidabad and Birbhum districts. However, Kanhu and his brothers refused to surrender as the British had expected and took the fight to them, winning small victories using guerrilla warfare and extending their reach gradually.

The British spread terror among their enemies. They moved swiftly, burning villages inhabited by Santhals without showing any sign of remorse. The Santhals suffered significant losses, but it was clear that the British were determined to end the war by any means necessary. For the East India Company, everything was about recovering their investment, so they couldn't afford to see their land burn.

Kanhu was now with the key commanders, including his brothers and sisters, Phulo and Jano. The Santhals had gathered in large numbers in a secluded part of the forest, equipped with bows, arrows, swords and a few guns. Kanhu spoke up, 'We must attack them to slow them down. My sisters have a plan.'

The warriors looked at Phulo and Jano, and Kanhu gave a gentle nod to his sisters, nudging them to go ahead. The two sisters stepped forward, touching the feet of some of the elder

Santhals and receiving their blessings.

Jano took the centre stage and said, 'This is our land. We have lived here for centuries, and we cannot let the British or their supporters take it. If we don't protect our space, we will soon have no space for us at all.'

The warriors listened intently, the only sound being that of the rustling leaves. Phulo looked towards the mountains and knew that the British were coming for them. Her thoughts were interrupted as Jano continued to speak, 'The British have spread their men all across, but we will never know peace if we don't stop them. We are fighting and winning but also losing some battles. However, it's only a matter of time before we take back our land. That can only happen if we continue to fight diligently.'

The Santhals began to chant their war cry, 'Hul! Hul! Hul!'

Phulo raised her hand and walked towards the centre. The warriors around her fell silent, eager to hear what she had to say. 'They are carrying out raids and destroying our homes. It's time for us to strike back by attacking them when they are asleep,' she said.

The sisters shared their plan to attack the British when they were most vulnerable—in a midnight raid. They planned to lead a group of women and raid the nearest British camps while the soldiers were sleeping, as they would attract less attention.

A moment of silence passed before one of the Santhal leaders spoke up. 'It is a bold idea,' he said.

Chand, worried for his elder sisters, added, 'But it is dangerous.'

Phulo knew this was true, but she also knew that they could not afford to rest. 'We cannot rest, my sisters and brothers. We must move forward,' Phulo said.

One of the leaders asked, 'Where shall we go? If we go outside and fight these men face to face, we will lose, for we are not strong enough.'

Phulo shook her head. 'We will fight them on our terms. We will attack them while they are asleep.'

The sisters explained their plan in more detail. Success would depend on the element of surprise. They kept the location of the targeted camp a closely guarded secret, but stated that a select group of men would follow them to provide cover during their escape. The tribe was energized by the plan. They would wait until the end of the day.

On the fateful night, hours passed and the moon had not yet reached its highest point. Phulo stepped out of her hut and looked at the resting warriors. She hoped for some respite. Kanhu was standing nearby, and Phulo told him the location of their target: Ganpur Bazaar and the nearby camp.

Kanhu was shocked. 'This is crazy, my sisters. Let me handle it,' he said.

Jano pointed to the sky. 'Many people said we were crazy for trying to regain our freedom and that the British would defeat us in days. But here we are, months later, still fighting. They cannot beat us. We have to keep up the fight.'

'Bold words. But this is still a dangerous idea, sister,' Kanhu said. He acted sceptically, not because he lacked trust in his sisters' abilities to complete the task, but because he couldn't bear the thought of losing more loved ones in the conflict.

'Return to us safely and don't fail. Do you hear me, Jano,

Phulo?' Kanhu issued an order, his tone firm but concerned.

'There's no way we'll ever fail, brother. You and father were the ones to train us,' Phulo replied.

As they reached the edge of the encampment, noticing the expression on Jano's face, Phulo asked her, 'What is it, my sister?'

'The moment we walk in like this, they'll recognize us. Even if we have the forest to hide us, we won't be able to keep our true identities a secret,' Jano replied, her voice filled with worry.

'Yes, you're right. Let's try to come up with a disguise,' Phulo suggested.

While the men needed time to rest and recover, Jano and Phulo volunteered to sneak into Ganpur Bazaar, an elite area where the moneylenders lived. Phulo sought the help of some Santhal warriors, asking for their assistance in obtaining garbs that would allow them to blend in when they went down to Ganpur Bazaar for the planned attack.

'Come, my friends, we will show you who we want to become.'

The warriors were excited to have something to do other than wait for the final battle. They followed the Murmu sisters deep into the dense forest, where the scent of the soaked earth following the previous day's rain still lingered. They didn't hurry but instead waited until they saw unsuspecting dikus dressed distinctively. They then signalled to a few Santhal men, who jumped out of hiding, covered the men's mouths, took their clothing and jewellery, and killed them.

Jano and Phulo's clothing was prepared with thick, wavy blue fabric. A tight, gold-coloured wrapping around their hips completed their disguise. It was snug, but good enough to allow them to blend in at Ganpur Bazaar. It wouldn't be easy for the authorities to single them out as Santhal women easily.

Jano said, 'Let's go. The sun is setting.' The two sisters moved quickly as the sun disappeared from the sky.

They reached the edge of their target, but everything was shrouded in darkness and they couldn't even identify the huts. The smell of roasted meat and charred wood reminded them of their lives before the war, when they cooked and ate together with their family.

Jano pointed in one direction and said, 'Let's split up and not get caught in the same place.' Phulo nodded, and they moved in opposite directions, brushing leaves aside.

Phulo gripped her dagger tightly. She couldn't let go of her fear. Speed was of the essence because they didn't want to be discovered, especially when they were alone.

Their bare feet made soft noises in the dirt as they approached the sleeping soldiers, whose snores and groans gave away their location. Phulo moved quietly over a form in the dim light, filtering through the leaves in the trees. She covered one man's mouth and quickly silenced him with a quick slash of her dagger across his throat.

Jano did the same, killing another man. They were making good progress—they had silently killed seven men so far without causing much disturbance.

The rustling of dry leaves shook their nerves, for it seemed that someone was awake. Phulo swung her spear, ready to attack. Jano, her muscles tense and her grip firm on her spear, sprang forward like a tigress, her eyes locked on the lantern. With a swift, powerful swing, she shattered it into pieces, sending shards of glass raining down onto the ground. The camp was plunged back into darkness, and confusion spread like wildfire among the disoriented soldiers.

Seizing the moment, Phulo charged towards the nearest enemy with her spear, each movement swift and precise. She struck him down before he could react, the sharp tip of her weapon finding its mark. As the soldier fell, cries of alarm began to ring out across the camp.

Phulo was unperturbed as she swung her spear at her enemies, bringing them down with unbridled violence. It was the manifestation of her rage.

Blood soaked into the soil as the enemies lay on the ground, some lying on the brink of death and others already dead—a final testament to their glory.

Jano got up from her crouched position and shook her arms, which were covered in blood. Splatters spotted Phulo's chest and arms.

The sisters fought side by side, their skill and ferocity unmatched by the unprepared British soldiers. Panic and chaos engulfed the camp, and the sisters' indomitable spirits only grew stronger, fuelled by their burning desire for justice and freedom. Their relentless onslaught sent the remaining soldiers fleeing into the night, their cowardice on full display.

As the dust settled and the sisters caught their breath, they looked around the now-empty camp, the aftermath of their daring assault a testament to their courage and resilience.

Jano looked around. 'Are they all dead?'

'Yes, they are,' Phulo replied.

Jano said, 'All of them will fall.'

Phulo slammed her axe into the neck of one of the dying men and he twitched. She wiped the blood from her forearm. 'They have to. If they don't fall, we will.'

A bird cooed in the darkness. Jano nodded as Phulo gestured for her to come closer. 'We need to leave before the sun rises.'

The two fled into the dark embrace of the forest. The bushes and the thick trunks of the trees concealed them from view and memory. The shouts and yells of the men they had killed became a fading memory as they ran, leaving the forest shaking with a lingering echo.

Like any other soldier, they were welcomed back with open arms. Their gasping breaths were their trophies, and the news of the twenty-one dead British soldiers and many more sepoys was their victory. Cheers of gratitude lifted the spirit of the Santhals and kept them focussed and ready for their next fight.

10 November 1855
Announcement of Martial Law
Santhal Land, Bharat

The government proclaimed martial law on 10 November 1855:

'It is hereby proclaimed and notified that the Lieutenant-Governor of Bengal, in the exercise of the authority given to him by Regulation X of 1804, and with the assent and concurrence of the President in Council, does hereby establish Martial Law in the following districts, that is to say: so much of the district of Bhagalpur as lies on the right bank of the river Ganges; so much of the district of Murshidabad as lies on the right bank of the river Bhagirathi; the district of Birbhum. And that the said Lieutenant-Governor does also suspend the functions of the ordinary criminal courts of judicature within the districts above described with respect to all persons, Santhals and others, owing allegiance to the British Government in consequence of their either having been born or being residents within its territories and under its protection, who, after the date of this Proclamation and within the districts above described, shall be taken in arms in open hostility to the said Government or shall be taken in the act of opposing by force of arms the authority of the same, or shall be taken in the actual commission of any overt act of rebellion against the state;

And that the same Lieutenant-Governor does also hereby direct that all persons, Santhals and others, owing allegiance to the British Government who, after the date of his Proclamation, shall be taken as aforesaid, shall be tried by Court Martial; and it is at this moment notified that any person convicted of any of the said crimes by the sentence of such court will be liable under Section 3, Regulation X of 1804, to the immediate punishment of death.'*

With this declaration, the British forces started to gain the upper hand. This law gave a free hand and encouraged the troops in the disturbed areas to attack the Santhals aggressively. The weather conditions, too, were now on their side, as the rainy season was over. Winters gave them more options for carrying out open military operations. In such operations, thousands of British troops attacked the Santhals and killed hundreds and thousands of them. The British could now destroy villages and jungles, and kill anyone they perceived as a threat. As with martial law, a shoot-at-sight order was passed. If a Santhal was seen, he or she was either killed or arrested and thrown into prisons.

---

*Datta, Kalikinkar, 'The Santhals Resurrection of 1855-57', Internet Archive, https://bit.ly/3HB3u7U. Accessed on 3 May 2023.

Early December 1855 to January 1856
Santhal Land, Bharat

The Santhals had been losing ground day by day, and the situation was reaching a point of no return. The loss of personnel, resources and land was pushing them back. Kanhu and the rest of the Santhal army knew they had to change their strategy to continue fighting. They started to attack in small bands, hoping to create shock and disruption while keeping to the forests.

The Santhals were not ones to back down. Even in the face of death, they stood firm, ready to fight and die with honour. In spite of their weariness, they refused to give up, fighting for their land and their people. On the other side, the sepoys were losing confidence with each skirmish. The back-and-forth battles began to tire the British officers and sepoys.

The Presidency Army, dressed in red coats and white pants, arrived with better weapons and more motivation. They were determined to end the war and crush the Santhals once and for all. The battles lasted for weeks, and the Santhals continued to fight with all their might. The British forces were shaken by the Santhals' unyielding determination.

As the war of attrition continued, the economic impact of

the suppression of the Santhals was becoming obvious for the British. The loss of agricultural production caused by the conflict was affecting both sides.

The Santhals knew they were running out of time, but they refused to give up. They fought with all their might, determined to crush their enemies and restore hope and faith in their land. The skirmishes continued. Only time would tell who would emerge victorious.

Kanhu rallied his people towards the Rajmahal Hills to make a bold move, gathering them from various spots in the jungle. The Santhals knew they were being followed by the Presidency's army. Several confrontations took place between the two sides. The British army, with its professional training and experience, did not press forward, but instead approached the base of the hill. It ended up giving the Santhals the advantage of high ground.

As the British fired their guns, attempting to break the formations of the Santhals, Kanhu refused to be intimidated. In spite the loss of their leader, the Santhals continued to shower arrows on their enemies, no matter the form of attack—be it through the power of the cavalry, the thundering of elephants shaking the earth or the use of bombs.

As the British raised their rifles, ready to fire, the Santhals did not let up on their volley of arrows. Kanhu stood on a tree branch, ready for what was to come. Suddenly, he noticed that the British had run out of ammunition. Kanhu saw an opportunity and raised his spear, leading a battle cry that echoed across the battlefield. The Santhals drew their swords and spears and rushed forward, eager to defeat the British.

The British army continued to retreat, breaking into smaller groups, with the Santhals in hot pursuit. As the Santhals entered the jungle, they became like a swarm of hungry bees, their thirst for blood only growing with each encounter. They approached the British army, who tried to defend themselves with cover fire from their artillery set at a distance.

The Santhals were not prepared for the unexpected barrage of bullets cutting through their ranks without hesitation. It was another trick from the British. Kanhu cried out in horror as he saw his younger brother Chand being shot in the head. The bullet went through his temple and exited through the back of his skull. Kanhu ran to Chand, knelt down and held his head in his lap, mourning his loss.

'Chaand...Chand,' Kanhu cried out.

The Santhal army crept forward through the thick jungle, communicating in hushed tones as they searched for the Presidency army soldiers. The firing that had stopped for a brief moment suddenly started again. Bullets whizzed through the air, striking the Santhals with deadly accuracy. They were confused and disoriented, unable to locate their enemy amidst the trees and shrubs.

'One of ours is hit! From the trees!' shouted a Santhal, realizing that the Presidency army had hidden men in the treetops. Panic spread through the ranks as the Santhals frantically searched for the marksmen, only to be pierced by bullets.

Kanhu, now the leader of the Santhals, was in shock and grief. He held his dead brother's head in his lap, tears streaming down his face. The firing intensified, and the Santhals looked to

Kanhu for command. But he was frozen, unable to think or act.

'Brother?' Bhairab appeared beside him.

Bhairab urged Kanhu to retreat, but as they tried to escape, the Santhal army was boxed in by artillery fire and bullets from the air. They were trapped, with no option but to push through the jungle.

As they fled, the Santhals stumbled upon a line of riflemen from the Presidency army. The British soldiers fired relentlessly, driving the Santhals back with each step. The Santhals were powerless to stop the onslaught.

The situation was dire and the Santhals were losing hope. Suddenly, there was a deafening explosion and a huge fire lit up the sky. The Presidency army had brought out their big guns, and any Santhal attempting to retreat was obliterated. It was clear that the only way out was to fight their way through.

Kanhu's mind raced, trying to make sense of the chaos surrounding him. He needed to quickly rally his army. With all his might, he shouted, 'Attack, attack!' And the Santhals repeated his call, the sound of their voices echoing through the jungle. The British continued to fire down upon them, but the Santhals refused to be deterred and pushed forward, their eyes fixed on their enemy. However, the Presidency army was prepared, and as the Santhals advanced, they were met with a hail of bullets. Blood spattered on the ground, and the Santhals fell, one after the other. Kanhu watched in horror as his comrades were killed before his eyes, their faces, throats, arms and legs riddled with bullets.

In spite of their best efforts, the Santhals were quickly

overwhelmed by the power of the Presidency army. Soon, the firing ceased as both sides stood still, facing each other. Kanhu's heart pounded in his chest as he heard the call to surrender, but he refused to give up without a fight. The Santhals charged forward once more, but it was a futile effort. More were killed and Kanhu, too, was injured.

The battle was catastrophic. When Kanhu finally regained consciousness, he saw the full extent of the damage. Almost five thousand Santhal men were now dead and the ground was stained with their blood.

Kanhu managed to escape into the jungle, but his heart was heavy with grief. As he looked back at the battlefield, he saw the lifeless bodies of his fellow Santhals lying on the ground, men, women and children alike. The sight filled him with anger and despair, and he turned and disappeared into the jungle, possibly for the last time.

There was an unlikely victim in the forest grieving the loss of a loved one. Major Vincent, too, had been a witness to the bloody battle. He sat with the head of a lifeless Santhal woman resting on his lap, his face emotionless. He gazed into her open eyes, and a tear rolled down his cheek, falling onto her face.

Mina. Oh, my Mina. My life is lost in my arms. My calmness gone forever. He closed his eyes and began to rock back and forth, feeling the weight of his grief. He could still see Mina standing by the riverbank, on the edge of the forest. He could see himself moving towards her through the thorny brush, the grass and the fallen leaves, feeling the pain of his bleeding feet. His dreams, too, had been plagued by the same visuals lately—a reminder of his failure to protect her from the violence of the rebellion.

'God was sending me a message,' he murmured to himself. 'I should have kept you safe. I should never have let you fight. Why did you have to fight?' He sighed heavily, feeling the weight of his guilt.

Then, Vincent noticed something at Mina's waist. It was something he recognized, as it had once belonged to him. He reached down and pulled out a small, tied bundle wrapped in a red cloth. As he opened the bundle, he saw the initials 'VJ' embroidered in gold. It was his handkerchief, the one he had lost, which Mina had taken and kept with her.

'You had a piece of me with you,' he whispered, his heart sinking further.

Vincent began to sob uncontrollably. He tried to compose himself as some of his men approached, telling him it was a victory for the British Empire, but he couldn't shake the feeling that it was a victory for cruelty, not humanity.

With a deep breath, he pulled himself together and stood up straight, smoothening his uniform jacket and holstering his pistol. He leaned down and gently kissed Mina's forehead, then turned and walked away without looking back.

In the following weeks, the Santhals continued to struggle against the might of the British Empire, losing crucial battles and valuable leaders to capture. The air was thick with a sense of impending doom and the streets were empty.

As the troops marched through the village, they tore aside the huts, revealing their wounded leaders. Minor skirmishes ensued,

SIDO KANHU

but the British troops quickly overpowered the Santhals, leaving no one alive. It was a devastating defeat for the Santhals and for Vincent, it was a reminder of the price one has to pay in wars.

January to February 1856
Somewhere in the Santhal Land

Kanhu sat on the cold, damp floor of his cell, his eyes closed as he tried to shut out the sights and smells that surrounded him. It had been weeks since the British had captured him and brought an end to the rebellion. The government had suspended martial law, and the British military had thoroughly suppressed the insurrection. Kanhu knew it was all over. However, he couldn't help but wonder about the fate of his people.

Without their leaders, most of the Santhals lost their enthusiasm for fighting. Kanhu knew that his capture would mark the end of the rebellion. The trial was swift, and he was aware that there was no hope for those who opposed the British Empire. He was going to be hanged. The struggle to free their homeland from British rule had been a long and difficult one, and it was true it would have been madness to think otherwise.

I guess this is it for me, Kanhu thought, feeling a sense of peace wash over him. He had stood up to the British and proved that his people were not weak. The future of his people was uncertain, but at least the children who had been spared from the tragedy would know that their ancestors did struggle for their freedom.

Kanhu and others had sacrificed everything for the good of others, even at the cost of their own well-being. Despite his self-loathing due to his perceived failures, he knew they had achieved more than they could have ever imagined. Their sacrifices were not in vain, as they had left an indelible mark in history.

As Kanhu's name was called out, he stepped forward to announce his identity and title. The executioner's voice boomed above the noise coming from the onlookers, and he noticed the soldiers surrounding the platform, rifles aimed at the crowd. His eyes met that of a soldier, but the latter slowly looked away.

A chill ran down Kanhu's spine, and he realized that it was his beloved brother, Bhairab. Everything started to become hazy, and he felt tears streaming down his face. He had done all he could for his people and those he loved, and there was nothing more left for him in this world. With no regrets in his heart, Kanhu was ready for what was to come.

His feet were shackled to the wooden platform, and as the executioner tied a rope around his neck and lifted him off the ground, he thought, 'Will my land ever be free again? Oh Thakur, please let my land be free.'

Kanhu struggled against the force pulling him down, not because he wanted to escape but because he wanted to show that he died a strong man. In spite of the pain of the rope cutting into his neck, he knew that one day, they would triumph over the British. His final thoughts before the trapdoor opened were of his homeland and his people. *I will see you all soon in the next life.* As the moment of his death approached, a flurry of emotions hit him. He closed his eyes and gasped, feeling the rope tighten around his neck. In spite of his vision blurring, he held himself upright, imagining Sido's face. He heard a snapping sound and soon his body went limp.

In his last moment, he saw a flash of light from far away. He opened his eyes again, and to his surprise, he saw Sido, beckoning him to come closer. At last, the two were at peace.

One year after the Hul
30 June 1856
Bangalore Cantonment

Vincent sat alone in his tent, his eyes misty with tears as he flipped through his diary. He could feel his heart heavy with the burden of the war that was unlike any other he had seen before. He couldn't shake the image of the enemy, standing firm, in spite of their bodies being pierced with bullets.

This is unlike any other war I have ever fought in. Our opponents do not understand surrender. They stand firm, even as our bullets rip through their bodies. Their arrows often take down our men, leaving us with no choice but to fire back as long as they stand. When their drums stop, they retreat a quarter of a mile, only to start the drumbeat again and stand calmly, ready to be fired upon once more. No sepoy in this war can escape feeling ashamed of himself, he read.

Vincent knew that he and his men were responsible for countless deaths, and he could hardly bear the guilt.

He put pen to paper. It was the only way he could unleash his innermost feelings. He wrote with a heavy hand, pouring out his heart and soul, detailing the atrocities he had witnessed. The Santhals, fierce and determined, had fought bravely, but it was clear that they could not match the might of the British Empire. Vincent could feel the shame of it all weighing heavily on his heart and he knew he could never forget what he had seen. He had to do something to ensure that the world would never forget the strength and determination of the Santhals—it was the only way to right the wrong in some way.

He paused for a moment, feeling the weight of the diary in his hands. He knew that some things were too terrible to write, even in diaries, but he couldn't help himself. He had to tell the story, so that the coming generations would know the truth. As he closed his eyes, Vincent saw the faces of the fallen, and he knew that he owed it to them to record what had happened.

With a deep breath, he gathered his strength and began to write his report. The words flowed freely, and he recounted his eyewitness account of the Santhals' heroic fight. He documented everything, not just the victories but also the horrors and the losses. He knew that this diary would become his personal mission to preserve the memory of the fallen and to honour their bravery.

As he wrote, he felt a sense of catharsis. He knew that he could not change the past, but he could help shape the future. He hoped that one day, his diary would be read by someone who would understand the true cost of war and the bravery of those who fought it.

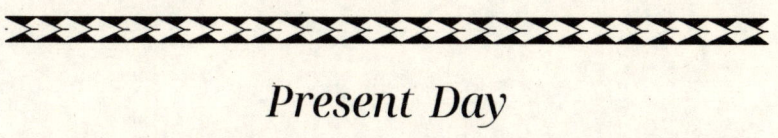
Present Day

Early June, present times
Charles Dickens Museum,
London, United Kingdom

The cardboard sign trembled in the hands of the bearded man wearing a monkey cap. His eyes scanned the indifferent faces of passersby as he held out his message of love. Suddenly, a thirty-two-year-old petite woman, with olive skin and a sunny smile approached him. Her yellow-and-white sundress swayed in the breeze as she reached out to embrace him, slipping a twenty-pound note into his hand. Overwhelmed with gratitude, tears sprang to his eyes as he returned the hug with all his might. As she pulled away, he saw hazel sparks in her eyes and felt a warmth emanating from her. She whispered encouraging words, patted his arm lightly and then disappeared around the corner, her dress swishing as she went.

Vanya Murmu stepped out onto the bustling streets of London, her dress paired with a fashionable shawl draped over her shoulders and gold bracelets encircling her wrists. Her long, braided hair cascaded down her back, and her dark olive skin glowed in the early morning sun. The scent of fresh bread mixed with coffee filled the air as she admired the city's iconic skyline.

As she made her way to the Charles Dickens Museum,

Vanya's captivating presence drew people in and pushed them away simultaneously, hinting at a complex and mysterious past. Her thoughts drifted to her father's sudden death while working in India, which had shattered her world and forever changed her.

She was now waiting nervously for a blind date arranged by her best friend. Her reluctance to date after a heart-wrenching break-up with a cardiac surgeon ten years her senior had finally given way to the hope of finding love again. As she stood outside the museum, her emotions were a mixture of excitement and trepidation. The day held endless possibilities, and Vanya was ready for whatever the future held.

I will go inside if he doesn't turn up soon. He is late.

James Jervis emerged from the depths of the Russell Square tube station in a burst of energy, his chest heaving and sweat trickling down his forehead. He stole a quick glance at his watch, realizing he was already thirty minutes behind schedule. In his haste, he barged past a middle-aged woman, nearly knocking her over.

The woman's face twisted into a scowl, and she hissed, 'You twat!'

James halted in his tracks, turning to face her with an apologetic smile. 'Sorry, Ma'am. I'm very late for a date. But you look beautiful,' he said, his blue eyes sparkling with charm.

The woman's sour expression melted into one of amusement, and she replied, 'Don't be late, but make sure you reach there in one piece.' James acknowledged her with a grateful nod before bolting towards the museum, his heart pounding with anticipation.

In spite of his privileged upbringing, James was acutely aware of the shackles of colonialism and the oppression that came with it.

He recognized the immense privilege that came with his position in society, and he felt a deep responsibility to use that privilege to effect positive change. His striking features—sandy blond hair and piercing blue eyes—drew attention. He felt confined by the expectations of his social status and craved to break out of his comfort zone to make a real difference in the world.

For tonight, he had been set up for a blind date by his friend Alhaadi Kenyatta. James was on his way to meet his date and venture into the unknown, excited but apprehensive about what awaited him.

As he approached the Charles Dickens Museum, his heart pounded even harder. He scanned the crowd for his date, looking for any sign of recognition. He spotted a petite woman by a wall, engrossed in an audio guide. He approached her, ready to offer his assistance, but before he could speak, the audio guide malfunctioned.

As she turned to face him, James recognized a familiar glimmer of recognition in her eyes. With an amused smile, she challenged him to impress her as her guide. James felt a surge of excitement and a hint of nervousness, ready to embark on this journey.

Vanya stepped into the adjacent room, and the first thing that caught her eye was the large dining table in the centre. James began to speak, his baritone filling the room as he told the story of Charles Dickens and his family, who had once lived in the very building they were standing in. Vanya listened intently as he pointed out the various cutlery and plates on the table, each labelled with the names of Dickens's friends, including his good friend Major Vincent Jervis, the nineteenth-century British officer.

As James spoke, Vanya couldn't help but be impressed by the warm and elegant atmosphere of the room. The simple yet stylish furniture, the big windows inviting natural light, and the golden-framed pictures adorning the walls, all contributed to the stunning ambience. James's stories were captivating, and she found herself drawn to his enthusiasm and knowledge.

When James paused, Vanya raised her hand to stop him. 'That will be all,' she said. 'We still need to formally introduce ourselves.'

James, standing a few inches taller than Vanya, smiled and introduced himself as a lawyer and history enthusiast, who hoped to become an author one day. Vanya, a medical resident training to become a surgeon, introduced herself in turn. As James heard about her profession, his blue eyes softened and a dimple appeared on his cheek as he replied, 'Ah, a pleasant surprise, Dr Vanya Murmu.'

As they made their way to another room, Vanya looked into James's eyes and felt a strange longing for companionship. He pointed to Charles Dickens's writing desk in the room. Vanya noticed a musty smell in the corner walls of the room as he spoke about his love for Dickens and his aspirations to write on the colonial history of Britain, particularly nineteenth-century India and the 1857 revolt.

Vanya was surprised to hear this and shared her own experience regarding Dickens. She said she started with *Oliver Twist* when she was a teenager in India and then read *Nicholas Nickleby*.

James told Vanya about his interest in colonial history, especially the events leading up to the 1857 rebellion in India and the lesser-known revolt of the Santhals in 1855. He explained how his ancestor had been a witness to those events, and how he now hoped to write a book about it one day. Vanya listened intently, impressed by James's passion for colonial history and his knowledge of the subject. She felt drawn to the way he spoke so eloquently about his interests, his easy smile and the way he made her feel completely comfortable.

He spoke with the authority of someone who had done his research, describing the events that led to the uprising and the impact it left on India's history. He spoke about his own family's connection to India, his eyes lighting up as he described their history as part of the trading community. Vanya furrowed her brow in concentration, eager to learn more about the tribe and their brave fight against the British.

As James spoke, she couldn't help but feel a sense of connection to the story. Her surname was Murmu. She realized that her ancestors might have been involved in the rebellion. She knew that her father who she had lost long ago was a Santhal, but she barely knew anything about the community. She realized she needed to find out more.

As they walked, Vanya found herself opening up to James about her father and the pain of losing him. Vanya spoke about how her father, an officer in the Indian Foreign Service, had passed away in India when she was just eight years old. James listened attentively, offering words of comfort and understanding.

Before they knew it, the sun started to set. They wandered

into a coffee shop. As they sipped their drinks and chatted, Vanya couldn't help but feel a sense of excitement. This was only the beginning of what seemed to be a promising and thrilling adventure, one that would perhaps take them both into the depths of India's history and even uncover a few secrets about their own families along the way.

As James reached into his bag, Vanya's curiosity was piqued. 'Would you like to read an old diary?' he asked, a hint of excitement in his voice.

Vanya leaned in and asked, 'Whose diary is it?' she asked.

'It belongs to one of my ancestors named Major Vincent Jervis, a great-great-great grandfather,' James replied, a smile spreading across his face.

Vanya's mind raced with possibilities. 'That must be over a hundred years old,' she remarked.

'More like over 165 years,' James corrected her. 'From the 1850s.'

Vanya gasped. 'From India's first war for independence?' she guessed, her eyes widening.

James nodded, impressed. 'My ancestor was an officer in the East India Company at the time.'

Vanya's interest wavered. 'I don't know whether it would interest me if it's just about war,' she said, wrinkling her nose.

James quickly reassured her. 'It's more of a human story,' he explained. 'Yes, there are war details, but it also provides a unique perspective of life in India at the time.'

Vanya considered it for a moment before nodding. 'Okay, I'll give it a try.'

James pulled out a well-worn, A4-sized diary, its pages yellowed with age. As he handed it to her, Vanya reverently ran her fingertips along the spine, amazed by the history she held in her hands. She noticed some sticky notes inside and asked about them. James explained that he used the diary as a reference text and asked her to not remove the notes. Vanya promised she wouldn't, and they shared a friendly laugh.

In the tube, she took out the diary, her heart racing with anticipation. She turned the pages, marvelling at the handwritten notes, knowing they contained a part of her past and perhaps her future. She came across a page with a post-it note stuck on it that read 'genesis'. Intrigued, she read the first line, 'It was the month of December 1852 in Kalikata…' and was immediately transported to a different world. As she delved deeper into the diary, Vanya couldn't wait to learn more about Major Vincent Jervis and colonial India. James had not only given her a glimpse into history but also into his heart. And with that, she knew a second date was due.

15 June, present times
A residence in Paddington
London, United Kingdom

Who am I? Did my ancestors really die such a painful death?

Vanya finished the first part of the diary. The diary ended with a familiar name. A name she recognized—Murmu. It talked about the battles fought by Sido and Kanhu Murmu.

My name is Vanya Murmu. Am I related?

She opened the diary again to have another look at its contents. And, there she read the words of Charles Dickens:

> There seems also to be a sentiment of honour among them [Santhals], for it is said that they use poisoned arrows in hunting, but never against their foes. If this be the case and we hear nothing of the poisoned arrows in the recent conflicts, they are infinitely more respectable than our civilised enemy, the Russians, who would most likely consider such forbearance as foolish, and declare that it is not war.*

Who were my ancestors? I need to go ask James for the next part. I need to go to India, and I need to go to Jharkhand.

---

*Household Works, Volume XII, p. 349, http://bit.ly/3pkPpFr. Accessed on 8 May 2023.

Vanya's grip tightened around the diary as she boarded the tube, trying to fight off the sense of aimlessness that plagued her. She flipped through the pages once more, her eyes tracing the faded ink, hoping to find some sort of direction. The tube jostled her body as it zipped through the tunnel, causing her to sway with the motion. She gazed at her reflection in the window and watched as the lights at each station illuminated her face before fading away. Her mind was in turmoil, consumed by the questions that had been gnawing at her for months. She felt torn between two worlds, neither of which seemed to fully accept her. Memories of long conversations with someone special filled her mind, briefly providing a respite from the constant struggle. But as the train pulled into the station and the doors slid open, Vanya was snapped back to reality.

The following morning, Vanya was finishing up a post-yoga shower when her phone rang. She ignored it at first, relishing the silence and the warm water that cascaded over her skin. But when it rang again, she reluctantly stepped out and checked the caller ID. It was James, the man she needed to talk to. She took the call.

'Good morning, Vanya. How was your night?' James's voice came through the speaker.

'Good morning, James. It was...fine. How was yours?'

'Just a quick trip to the office, but I slept well. All okay?'

Vanya hesitated, trying to figure out how to broach the topic. 'There's something,' she finally said. 'Can we talk later?'

James let out a sigh. 'Sure,' he said before hanging up.

Vanya's heart sank into her stomach as she stood in the bathroom, staring blankly at her phone. She couldn't understand what was wrong with her. Had she missed something significant? She wracked her brain, trying to recall any events from the previous day that could have acted as a reason of concern. But there was nothing she could single out as a possible reason, and the unease lingered like a dark cloud over her head.

Vanya's fingers itched to dial James's number as she sat at her desk, the diary lying unopened beside her. She picked up her phone and hit the call button, but it went straight to voicemail. Her frustration grew as she dialled his number four times, each time with no response. Finally, James picked up the call, his voice filled with amusement. Vanya tried to hide her annoyance as he asked about the diary. She confirmed that she had read it.

The need to learn about her heritage burnt within her and Vanya knew that she needed to search for her past. James offered to bring another diary to lunch. It carried Major Vincent Jervis's reflection after the 1855 Santhal battles once he was back in England, he said. They set a time to meet at the British Museum.

Vanya settled into her seat, deep in thought. Vanya thought about the Santhal tribe and how they were hunted down by the British. She wondered what were Sido's views on freedom and balance with nature. She also had questions about her own heritage.

20 June, present times
A residence in Paddington
London, United Kingdom

As Vanya read Major Vincent Jervis's nineteenth-century diary, she felt a deep connection to her ancestors. She sat on her balcony, sipping her chamomile tea. She thought about the pain and history contained within the diary, and how it was both something to remember and be proud of.

As a flock of seagulls flew by, chirping loudly, Vanya's mind wandered to a book she had read about fate and choice. She thought about Sido, her ancestor, who believed in both fate and choice, and how his decisions had brought their tribe together. But did she feel connected to them?

As the birds fell silent and the sounds of the city went down, Vanya went inside and looked at a photograph of herself standing triumphantly on a cliff. She remembered the challenge and how it was all worth it to reach the summit. The old photos of her family and friends made her feel content.

Sitting on her bed, she gazed around her familiar room, contemplating if she had done everything for herself and if there was more she could do for her lost ancestors. She knew that the words in Major Vincent Jervis's diary carried more depth, which was something she needed to delve into.

She looked at the diary again, realizing that those words would live on forever if they were to be passed down. Vanya's ancestors had taken fate into their hands and changed their destiny, and now she felt a need to be with them, to learn from them, to help them.

Looking at herself in the mirror, Vanya felt that it was time to search beyond her own needs and embark on a journey to India to pay homage to her ancestors.

A few weeks later, James drove Vanya to the airport, where he dropped her off at the entrance of the departure. They hugged each other tightly before she walked towards the airport, only to turn back once and wave a goodbye. After going through the checks and clearances, Vanya put on her headphones and listened to some Santhali music, checking the flight announcement signboard every now and then.

Finally, she saw her flight details on the big screen and made her way to her window seat. She fastened her seat belt as the cabin door closed behind her, and the captain announced that they were about to take off. As the plane lifted off the ground, Vanya leaned against the window and watched as the city lights of London spread out below her.

Feeling nervous, excited and happy, all at once, Vanya noticed two planes flying side by side, one with an emblem of a lion on its tail. She glanced at her watch and saw that it was 4.00 p.m. She felt tired and decided to nap. When she woke up, the cabin lights were dimmed, and she saw clouds outside the window, accompanied by lightning flashes.

As the plane turned east and climbed rapidly, Vanya looked at the sky, feeling a sense of adventure. She couldn't help but think about the tribes she had read about in the book her mother had given her and how they would do anything to protect their home. The stewardess asked if she wanted tea or coffee, but Vanya shook her head, lost in her own thoughts. She was starting to feel tired again. It was time for another nap.

'Vanya, dear Vanya. I have never felt so happy about anything as I do about you coming to visit me,' a voice called out to her.

She spun around, trying to locate the source of the voice. Her eyes fell on the endless horizon, and she saw nothing but darkness.

'Am I dreaming?' Vanya murmured to herself, not sure what to believe.

'Yes, Vanya, you are dreaming,' the voice replied, 'But it might also not be a dream.'

Vanya looked around, feeling like she was in another time and a faraway place. A sense of both excitement and apprehension filled her as she tried to make sense of the voice's cryptic words.

'Who is it?' she asked, her voice barely above a whisper.

'You know who this is,' the voice replied.

'Sido...Sido Murmu?' Vanya called out, her voice echoing across the empty expanse.

Suddenly, a heavenly figure appeared in front of her, surrounded by blinding light. As the light faded away, Vanya saw the figure of a man. He was tall and muscular, his skin a rich shade of brown. His eyes were unblinking, and they seemed to bore into her soul.

'Sido,' Vanya breathed, taking a step towards him.

She fell to her knees, touching the ground at his feet before rising to stand next to him. She could feel the heat radiating from his body, and she was drawn to his unblinking gaze.

'*Vanya, when you visit my place, find a way to spread my story,*' *Sido said, his voice filled with urgency.*

'*How?*' *Vanya asked, her heart racing in her chest.*

'*You will see and hear,*' *Sido replied, his form shimmering before fading away.*

Vanya jolted awake, feeling disoriented and confused. She remembered the dream vividly and a shiver ran down her spine. Did she get a message from her ancestor? What did he mean by finding a way to tell his story ahead?

She couldn't shake off the feeling that something significant was about to happen, and it filled her with a sense of excitement and dread. Vanya knew that her journey to India was not going to be a simple vacation. There would be more to it than that.

~

30 June, present times
Dumka, Jharkhand

Vanya's heart raced with excitement as she arrived near the Sido Kanhu Murmu University. The previous twenty-four hours of travelling had been nothing short of a whirlwind, but no obstacle could dampen her spirit. She stepped out of the car, taking in the sight of the memorial park, with its vast open space and towering trees. The chirping of birds filled the air, and Vanya closed her eyes, savouring the sense of belongingness at last.

But as she explored the park, she couldn't shake the feeling that something was amiss. She yearned for a deeper connection. So, she changed her plan and hired a local driver, a Murmu like herself, who knew the history of the place.

As they drove out of the city, the world transformed around them. The wide roads gave way to narrow and winding ones, and soon, they were on a dirt road, with only the distant sounds of the city keeping them company. Vanya was lost in her thoughts, listening intently to the stories of her ancestors as they wound their way to the village. She wanted to visit a village near the university.

When they finally arrived, it was like stepping into a different time altogether. The village was a sight to behold, surrounded by lush green hills, brick houses and huts. Animals roamed freely, and Vanya couldn't help but smile at the sight.

As she walked towards a large house, Vanya felt quite excited. She wondered if the people inside were related to her in some way or the other. The sound of laughter and chatter greeted her, and she saw a group of people on the first floor, enjoying refreshments.

Vanya approached the door and knocked, her heart pounding with anticipation. A few seconds later, a man opened the door, smiling at her. A little girl holding his hand looked up at Vanya with wide eyes, eager to see who had come to visit them.

'Hi, my name is Vanya. I am here to visit the Sido Murmu Memorial.'

The man smiled widely and the little girl started jumping with joy. Vanya felt amused by their reaction.

'I too am Vanya!' the little girl sang out loud, and all three of them burst into laughter. The man welcomed Vanya and invited her inside. She felt at home and trusted the occupants of the house instantly.

As she made her way up to the first floor, she saw several pairs of eyes watching her every move. She felt self-conscious, but it was not for long. Suddenly, a feminine voice broke the silence, calling out her name. She turned to see a woman lying on a cot with a little boy beside her. Vanya greeted the woman with the customary tribal salutation.

Vanya moved on to talk to the other people in the room, including an old man and woman, and three adults. The last person she spoke to was the great-grandmother of the little girl who had greeted her at the door. The woman's voice was frail, and Vanya felt her heart swell with compassion for her. She squatted down beside the old lady and held her hands.

'I knew you would come,' the old woman said, speaking in Santhali language. Vanya only understood a bit and the rest was translated to her. She felt blessed as the old woman placed her hand on her head.

'Sido told me she would come,' she said out loud.

The people in the house heard this and smiled, explaining to Vanya that they keep seeing visions of Sido from time to time and consider it a blessing. The man who had opened the door for Vanya said that his grandmother had predicted that a visitor from far away would come someday, but also kept insisting it would be a girl with a name familiar to them.

As Vanya sat with the old woman, a group of young people gathered outside. They were there to take her to the memorial, and the little girl wanted to go with her. Vanya picked up the little girl and walked outside, where she saw children playing, laughing and running around.

Outside, Vanya came across a girl who greeted her, revealing her pearly white teeth, and introduced herself as Mina. As they shook hands, Vanya asked her, 'We're going to the memorial, would you like to join us?'

'Of course,' Mina replied, and they set off on their journey. After walking for about fifteen minutes, they could hear the distant sound of a river. The lush green jungle was in full view. Vanya took in her surroundings, hearing the sound of the river growing louder as they approached the memorial statue of Sido and Kanhu.

As they reached the riverbank, Vanya was awed by the force of the river. The sweet aroma of the fields filled her nostrils, and she felt a sense of peace wash over her. This was the place where her ancestors had grown up, where they had fought their battles, standing up to the colonial powers. In spite of their struggles in the past, the Santhals' culture still thrived.

Turning towards the memorial, Vanya was met with the statues of two men, their faces etched with pain, anger and sorrow. As she gazed at the figures, she felt the pain of the soldiers resonate within her.

The sun was high in the sky, causing her to sweat profusely. She felt the warm breeze caress her skin. The grass beneath her feet was nothing but soothing. The air was calm and serene.

Vanya was lost in thought, standing there for what seemed like an eternity before reluctantly leaving for her hotel. Suddenly, a voice jolted her back to reality. 'It's good that you've come here, Vanya. This place hasn't been visited by outsiders for many years,' the voice said.

Vanya turned around and saw two men standing behind her, both dressed as city dwellers. One of them looked familiar, and as she squinted her eyes, she asked, 'Do I know you? You look familiar.'

The familiar man smiled at her and said, 'Hi, my name is Tuhin.'

Vanya asked, 'Tuhin?'

'Tuhin Sinha,' he replied.

'Ah, yes. The author. I just read your book, *The Great Tribal Warriors of Bharat*,' said Vanya.

'Thank you. Your mother contacted us and mentioned that you would be coming here, so we thought we'd surprise you,' Tuhin chuckled. 'Ah, before I forget, this is my friend and fellow author, Suraj, who goes by the pen name of Clark Prasad.'

Suraj greeted Vanya. Tuhin continued, 'We are actually here for different reasons, but we have one thing in common here.'

Vanya nodded and smiled, 'Sido and Kanhu.'

'Yes, Sido Murmu and Kanhu Murmu, the entire Murmu family and the entire Santhal community who stood up for what was right,' replied Tuhin.

'True, we need to do something,' said Vanya, turning around and looking at the flowing river.

'Vanya, we will tell their story to the world,' said Tuhin. 'Let us now go to the university. The students are waiting.'

AFTERWORD: IMPACT OF THE HUL

As the Santhal uprising drew to a close, Ashley Eden, who would later rise to power as the lieutenant governor of Bengal, was tasked with uncovering the reasons behind the surprising rebellion. To his and the government's shock, Eden discovered the truth about the Santhals' grievances. The lack of an effective judicial system and the mere collection of taxes without any benefits in return were the root causes of the uprising.

With this newfound knowledge, the Santhal Parganas Act (Act XXXVII) of 1855 was introduced, consolidating the Santhal territories into a distinct non-regulation district known as the Santhal Parganas. The district was separated from Bhagalpur and Birbhum and divided into four sub-districts: Dumka, Deoghar, Godda and Rajmahal. Eden, who was appointed as the first deputy commissioner of Santhal Parganas, introduced the Police Rules of 1856, granting the manjhis of Santhal villages to act in the capacity of policemen in their communities with the assistance of the village chowkidar.

The law finally caught up with the corrupt moneylenders who exploited the Santhals, leading to an end of the fraudulent practices of charging the same debt multiple times, bonded labour and slavery, along with the manipulation of weights and measures. With these reforms, the Santhals were able to sell their produce without fear of being cheated.

However, the greatest impact of the Hul revolution was the unity it brought to the Santhals living across Damin-i-koh and the Santhal Parganas. The rebellion brought the people together in their quest to build their promised land and protect their cultural identity.

As we look back on the Hul revolution and its impact on the Santhals, we are left to ponder the cost of neglecting the voices of the marginalized and the power of the people to rise against injustice. The story of the Hul is a reminder for all of us to strive for a better world where everyone's rights are protected and their voices are heard.

ACKNOWLEDGEMENTS

I am grateful to my co-author Suraj Prasad (Clark) for believing wholeheartedly in my vision. His perspicacious research and writing efforts on *Mission Shengzhan* and *Sido Kanhu* are truly priceless. I do hope that one day these books are remembered for their true worth.

I'd like to thank my publisher and friend Kapish Mehra for always being so hands-on and supportive. A special thanks to the brilliant Rupa team: Mr A.K. Singh, Yamini, Aurodeep, Swar, Vasundhara and Geetu.

I am grateful to my better half, Koral, son, Neev, and my Dad for all their love and support. My Mom continues to inspire me even after her death.

Last but not the least, I'd like to thank my legacy of readers and well-wishers nurtured over 17 years of diligent experimentation with myriad genres and stories. With your support and love, I will keep striving to raise the bar.

Tuhin A. Sinha

First and foremost, I am eternally indebted to Tuhin A. Sinha, who entrusted me with the responsibility of collaborating on this significant project. Our collective efforts have taken us on an extraordinary voyage of self-discovery, and the lessons I have learnt along the way are truly priceless. I want to give a big thanks to the team at Rupa Publications for making this dream come true.

I am grateful to my parents, Dr Janardan Prasad, formerly a captain in the Army Medical Corps, a 1971 war veteran and General Service Medal recipient, and Savitri Prasad, former lieutenant of the Military Nursing Service. I am indebted to them for their unwavering support, sacrifices and guidance they have provided throughout my life. Amma, your absence leaves an irreplaceable void, but I am resolute in fulfilling the potential you recognized and nurtured within me.

My wife, Vidya K.S., deserves a special mention for her loving nature and strength. In the darkest moments of doubt and turmoil, you have been my beacon of hope and my steadfast pillar of support. Your constant encouragement has been the driving force behind my every endeavour.

To my fellow writers, I urge you to persist in crafting your stories and sharing your insights. Our words possess the power to ignite change and inspire others to reach for the stars. In the maze of life, it is often the wisdom and illumination from those around us that lead us towards our destinies. May our writing stand as a testament to the power of resilience, adaptability and the indomitable human spirit.

Suraj Prasad